Bea *and the* NEW DEAL HORSE

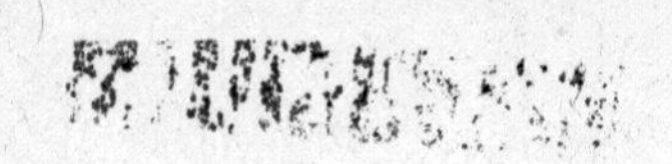

Bea and the NEW DEAL HORSE

L. M. ELLIOTT

This book is a work of fiction. While the historic, contextual facts of the Great Depression are real, the characters and their dialogue in this novel are products of the author's imagination.

Katherine Tegen Books is an imprint of HarperCollins Publishers.

 For information address HarperCollins Children's Books, a division of HarperCollins Publishers, 195 Broadway, New York, NY 10007.
www.harpercollinschildrens.com

Library of Congress Control Number:
ISBN 978-0-06-321900-7

Typography by Carla Weise and Andrea Vandergrift
23 24 25 26 27 LBC 5 4 3 2 1
❖
First Edition

To Peter and Megan, the bravest, most
straight-to-the-fence souls I know.
To our Aunt Ann, who, seventy years
later, still hears the music of her
favorite horse cantering through fields.
And in memory of Megan's cantankerous,
lionhearted champion, Mullingar, who loved
her and would take any jump *for her*; and
graceful Connor, a wondrous handful of a
different sort, who won a pony club nationals
with her and her Virginia teammates.

"I don't think she [Ginger] does find pleasure in biting," said Merrylegs; "it is just a bad habit; she says no one was ever kind to her, and why should she not bite?"

—Anna Sewell, *Black Beauty*

I pledge you, I pledge myself, to a new deal for the American people. . . . In these days of difficulty, we Americans everywhere must and shall choose . . . the path of hope, and the path of love toward our fellow man.

—President Franklin Delano Roosevelt

CHAPTER 1

I woke up in a billowing pile of fresh-cut hay, wrapped in its miraculous smells—of buttercups, of those miniature fuzzy wild daisies, of grasshoppers. Not the big, prickly legged locusts that spit tobacco juice but the sweet little sliver of green grasshoppers that look like tiny blades of grass. No needles of dried-up, dead-yellow straw sticking and tickling either. Soft, like sleeping on a little mountain of emerald-colored lace.

So very different from the harsh coal-stink and hard wooden planks of the railcars Daddy had had us hopping the previous weeks.

I snuggled deeper into the green, trying to hang on to its feel of happy, drowsy sunshine, lullabied by the slow, steady breathing of horses slumbering beneath the hayloft where I was lying with my little sister and father. A sound I had grown up on and now ached for, ever since the stock market crashed and Daddy had had to sell off most every scrap of our previous life, including Mama's mare and my Dandy Boy. How I missed that fun-loving, good-natured pony. He would have lain down right next to me, content in this sweet, fresh hay.

I rolled over and put a protective arm on Vivian, wondering if she missed Dandy, too. She squirmed against my hug. Viv's got to be the world's most contrary eight-year-old, I swear. It would be a task to keep her quiet when she woke. And we'd need to be. Given how Daddy had slipped us into the barn at night, guided only by moonbeams spilling through the enormous open doors of the stable's center aisle, we clearly were supposed to be hiding.

I was growing more accustomed to our vagabond life—well, trying to be. We'd bedded down in so many barns now, just for the night, leaving before their owners got up in the morning, on our way to wherever Daddy thought he could find work. But this felt different—he'd brought us to this stable specifically. Why, I didn't know.

The hard fact was each day and what it might hold had become a total mystery for the past two years since Daddy's bank had closed and laid him off. Like so many Americans since the Great Depression fell on us like a plague, he'd tried to make do with odd jobs. But a man who'd spent his adult life in three-piece suits and bow ties overseeing bank accounts for Richmond's old society didn't easily transition to being a handyman or tobacco picker. To say Daddy didn't know his way around a hammer or a hoe is what Mama would have called the understatement of the century.

Mama. What would Mama say to Daddy to get him out of the flask of outlawed whiskey he carried with him now? Stuff made from God knows what in some yokel's back woodshed. It wasn't Daddy's fault that everyone's money evaporated like a small puddle in the noonday sun. But some days I just wanted to scream at him to be the daddy he used to be. The least he could do is keep his head straight.

I opened my eyes. Dawn was seeping into the barn in warm ribbons of rose light. I followed its glow. Directly above me, up in the eaves, was a barn swallow's nest, a deep balcony sculpted of mud and sticks. I hadn't spotted that wonderment in the night's darkness. As I marveled, its maker wriggled out of her cleverly daubed nest, warbled a good morning at me, and, in a flash of cobalt blue and cinnamon, dove and swooped through the open doors, disappearing into the bright-gold sunshine.

I actually heard air brushing along the swallow's feathers as she skated right by me in such a friendly hello. That gorgeous bird coming so close—like she was making sure I was all right—had to be a good omen. Had to be. Mama always read all sorts of meaning into birds. Maybe we could stay put for a while. For a few days anyway. *Please, Daddy.*

Below, the horses shuffled and snorted, waking

up as well, giving little expectant nickers, watchful for their breakfast. Someone would be coming to feed them soon. My grip on Viv tightened, anticipating having to put a hand over her mouth just as—in the clockwork that is a good barn—someone entered whistling softly. I held my breath. It'd break my heart to be discovered and chased away like a stray dog from this heavenly place.

Mercifully, Viv stayed asleep through the scoop and dump of grain into seven feed tubs and the answering chorus of methodical munching.

The scent of molasses drifted up to me. Sweet feed! Oat, corn, and barley grain mixed and moistened with thick, delicious molasses. I almost drooled remembering the taste of pancakes covered with that heavy dark brown syrup.

"Enjoy, children," a male voice crooned to the horses. "Be back in a few to turn y'all out." Footsteps faded away.

"Someone's coming back soon," I whispered in Viv's ear. "Stay quiet."

She kicked out at me. "Let me sleep, Bea. I'm so tired."

"You do that." I pulled her sweater up tighter around her and patted her shoulder before sitting up to stretch. My own stomach was growling with hunger that would have rattled me out of slumber. I was amazed hers wasn't as well.

But the journey had been an exhausting one—clambering into a freight car just outside Norfolk. Hiding for hours in smelly darkness with an old gentleman and his frightened wife, who'd also become unlikely, Wall Street–made nomads. *Clank-clank, clank-clank*, the careless lurching of a delivery train not worried about discomforting passengers since there were no paid ones. Passing by Manassas and climbing out at The Plains, then walking, hitching, walking, hitching until we arrived here around midnight.

Wherever here was. Somewhere a little north of a place called Middleburg. Dropped off on the side of a dirt road by a man who gave us a lift in what he called his Hoover-cart—a car stripped down to its chassis because he couldn't afford gas, pulled by a pair of thoroughbreds obviously unused to the task. We'd staggered up a brutally long lane past a sign that read: Galashiels Glen. Daddy had had to carry Vivian at that point.

Sleep would do her good.

Better wake Daddy, though, before the stable hand returned, since he did snort and snore in his sleep. And lately Daddy tended to groan as he woke, holding his head. Sometimes he even retched, spontaneous with opening his eyes, as if poison had been percolating in him all through the night and had just reached the boiling point. Any of which would be a dead giveaway to someone below. I looked over to where Daddy had bedded.

I didn't see him.

He'd probably gone outside to relieve himself. Daddy did that plenty when we were on the move. Or maybe he'd burrowed down deep into the cloud-bank of hay like I had. I stood to better see into his corner. "Daddy? You awake?" I whispered.

Nothing.

"Daddy, where are you?" I called quietly.

No answer.

Vivian flopped and muttered, "Shhh. Don't wanna get up."

Kneeling, I put my hand on her once again to silence her. Where *was* Daddy? I turned to look toward the ladder, hoping to see him coming back up it. A creepy-crawly anxiety was starting to swarm me.

That's when I realized Daddy's knapsack was missing.

Then I spotted one of his monogrammed handkerchiefs, knotted tight into a little bundle, to hold and protect something. Placed atop my small suitcase—so it would be the first thing I saw. My hands started trembling so much I couldn't untie the knot. I finally tore at the handkerchief with my teeth to loosen it, tasting a tiny leftover hint of bleach from long ago and fighting back an anxious sob.

Inside was a short note scrawled with a dull pencil nub, making it all thick and smeared. The handwriting looked shaky. Not Daddy's bank-officer penmanship at all.

My darling Beatrice and Vivian, the lady who owns this estate—a Mrs. Scott—is the mother of your mama's roommate at Sweet Briar College. They were good friends once. Her roommate's name is Marjorie. Ask for her at the house. Tell her you are Cora's girls. I'm sure she or her mother will take you in and take good care of you, the way I cannot now. Your mama always said they had good hearts.

I read his words again, convinced I'd skimmed them wrong. And again. And again. My vision getting blurrier each time. Daddy couldn't mean it. He couldn't. But at the bottom, he'd scratched out *~~Forgive me~~* and replaced it with *I do this because I love you.*

Daddy had left us. Dumped us, like unwanted kittens by the side of a highway with the hope a passing stranger would take pity on them.

How could he do this?

Folded inside the scrap of paper were the only items of Mama's he'd been able to keep: a beautifully etched gold locket and her wedding ring. And a small photograph of the four of us when

Vivian was a baby, tucked into an envelope, its silver frame long sold.

I retched—dry-heaving over that beautiful bed of hay, ruining my corner of it with spittle.

Like father like daughter, I guess.

CHAPTER 2

If I could have willed myself to die and join Mama at that moment, I think I might have. But Viv suddenly sat up. "Bea, I'm hungry," she whimpered. "Really hungry." She rubbed her eyes and glanced around. "Where's Daddy?"

I stared at my little sister for a beat. A long one. "Gone to look for work." The lie popped out of my mouth. No need to terrify Viv. To break her heart, too. Not if I could help it. Not yet. I stuffed the note and Mama's precious jewelry into my pocket, with a curse under my breath about my father that

I shouldn't repeat if I ever hope to be a lady.

Viv sighed. "Do we have anything to eat?"

"A couple of biscuits left and some powdered milk."

Her golden brown eyes got big—I mean gigantic. I swear when that child is not a whirling dervish, she's about the most pitiful little thing there is.

"That's all?"

I made myself smile at her. "I bet there're some carrots in the feed room below."

"Oh, goody." Vivian pretended to clap her hands. "Maybe some chocolate, too? Or ice cream?"

Where she picked up sarcasm I'll never know. Mama had forbidden it as being mean-spirited. Had Vivian's statement not been mixed with such wistfulness, I might have feared my baby sister was already long-gone bitter, before even reaching a decade of age. Hunger and constant unknowns can do that to a child.

Making myself stick to playful to pull Viv and me in that direction, I mimicked the maître d' at the elegant Jefferson Hotel where we used to go after church for Sunday lunch. "The chef is not in yet, mademoiselle," I said in a deep voice. "But perhaps I can bring out an apple for your enjoyment." I tugged gently on her ear. "Let me go look."

I fake-smiled again, although I was quaking inside, knowing how easily I might get caught. Would the local sheriff throw a thirteen-year-old into the hoosegow for stealing from a feed bin? I couldn't help but remember the group of teenage hobos riding the rails looking for work—one of them a girl disguised as a boy—who talked about the meanness of "bulls"—the railroad company detectives who patrolled railyards and trains armed with rifles and billy clubs. "Ever been chased in a field by a bull hell-bent on skewering you on his horns?" The girl had said, nodding meaningfully.

Worried about them, Daddy had asked why they'd left home.

"Farm went under," answered the teenager who seemed to be their leader. "Pop couldn't make our mortgage. Bank foreclosed." Daddy had winced at that. "Couldn't feed us neither. My aunt offered to take us in. All four of us. So that Pop and Ma could go to the city to find work. Ma's a good seamstress." The boy sighed. "But my aunt has her own kids, little ones. I'm old enough to fend for myself. I didn't want to be the extra burden."

At the time, given his puckered expression, I'd wondered if Daddy might cry. I assumed he was feeling guilty about what the bank had done. I knew he'd had to foreclose on houses himself before his bank folded. But maybe that's where he got the bass-ackwards idea of leaving us—the story of that aunt taking in four hungry children.

Well. I'd just have to be like that train girl now—hide my fearful, hurt self in the clothes of practicality. Zip closed my feelings. Find a way to feed us until I figured out what to do next.

I did a quick calculation. The man who'd fed the horses was surely on his way back to let them out soon. He was probably just filling their paddock troughs with water. That meant maybe twenty minutes for my raid. *Move, Beatrice. Don't be a scaredy-cat.* It wasn't like I was trying to jump up into a moving train, like those teenagers had dared. All I was looking at was a ladder.

I swung my feet onto its first rung and scrambled down.

As soon as I touched the aisle floor the horses' heads bobbed up, ears pricked. They started that lovely whickering horses make when they're curious about something that's just appeared. My heart skipped a little, remembering Dandy Boy's greeting—his happy whinny—when he spotted me. Not many horses are that affectionate. Sleek, muscular creatures made to gallop free, fast as winds—many just tolerate us paltry humans and what we ask of them. Others can be outright aloof. So when a horse truly loves his rider, lights up when he spots her, delights in what she asks and the jumps they take together, lends his strength and speed to her so she feels like she's flying—that kind of partnership? Well, gosh. It's beyond magical. Dandy Boy was like that.

And my father had sold him.

I knew he had to. But I couldn't help worrying

about Dandy's new home. I'd read *Black Beauty*. I knew not all horse people were kind.

"Carrots," I whispered aloud to make myself move.

Even though my worries about the stable hand coming back made me want to dart, I walked cautiously down the bank of stalls, almost tiptoeing. Rushing would set the horses off. Wolves being one of their natural predators, quick movements make them nervous. When they're really startled or riled, they lash out with their hooves and neigh loudly. If the stable hand's hearing was good, and there was even the slightest commotion coming from the barn, he'd know something unusual was inside, worrying the horses.

"Hey, fellas," I crooned low as I passed two bright-eyed, almost identical bays side by side, then a roan, an onyx and very round mare, and two dappled-grays. They all held their muzzles up to the stall bars looking for a treat, their huge nostrils quivering as they took in my smell. "Sorry, I don't have anything for you," I murmured as I passed.

The tack and feed rooms were down at the end of the aisle. It was a big barn, ten spacious stalls each on either side—but more than half were empty. So I was surprised when I came to the last one to see a tall, lean chestnut, separated from all the other horses. Rump toward me, he was looking out his window that opened to the pastures and hills beyond. As I passed, he turned to assess me for just a moment before returning his severe gaze back to the outside world. His disdain for me—or was it a defensive what-do-*you*-want?—sent a strange shiver through me.

Opening the door to the tack room, the familiar smell of well-rubbed leather and cedar paneling embraced me. Dozens of saddles and bridles hung on the walls. Fleecy saddle pads were stacked atop one another. Tack boxes I knew would be full of bootjacks, spurs, brushes, currycombs, and hoof picks lined the floor. Everything was lacquered with more than the usual amount of stable dust. Clearly, this room and its tack hadn't been used in a while.

In the feed room, I found what I was hoping

for. Inside the bin of grain were tin buckets filled with carrots and dried apples. There was enough that I could stuff my pockets with both without it being obvious someone had raided the supply. The horses might not be being ridden, but they were being fed well.

As I closed the bin's heavy wooden lid and latched it—I knew better than to leave it open to field mice—I heard whistling.

My heart stopped—then started galloping. He was back. I looked around frantically. No place to hide. If the stable hand came into the feed room, he'd catch me—pockets full.

The whistling turned to singing a slowed-down version of a ragtime tune. *Yes, sir, that's my baby . . .*

Could I manage to slip out the door and into the field before he saw me?

No, sir, don't mean maybe . . .

That wouldn't work. I'd spook that haughty chestnut if I opened the door and bolted.

Yes, sir, that's my baby now . . .

Could I climb into the bin itself? No, too full.

Yes, ma'am, we've decided . . .

My only hope was that he wouldn't come into the feed room. Or if he did, to cower behind the door as it opened—like some ridiculous slapstick Laurel and Hardy moving picture.

No, ma'am, we ain't gonna hide it . . .

Oh my God. What about Vivian, I thought. Please stay quiet, Viv, for once in your life. I clapped my hands to my mouth as if silencing me would dampen her.

Yes, ma'am, you're invited now. The singing stopped. "How you doing this fine morning, honey. Ready to go out?"

I heard the sound of a heavy stall door rolling back along its rails. The rattle of a halter being taken off its hook and slipped over a horse's head, the click of a lead line being attached to its ring. A slow *clop-clop-clop-clop* as the horse stepped into the aisle.

The other horses starting pacing and snorting, impatient to be freed too.

"All right, all right, young'un. You too." Rattle. Click. An antsy, dancing *clip-clip.*

"The rest of you boys behave until I come back. Ya hear?"

The stable hand was walking out the horses two at a time. Here was my chance. I could dash back up the ladder as he made the trip to the pasture and back. I listened to hooves echoing down the aisle and then turning quiet as they hit grass. Now!

I opened the tack room door and peeped around its edge. The stable hand was thin and wiry, slightly hunched with old age, with a limp that had probably come from a horse kick or fall sometime in his life. I watched him retreat and then trotted to the ladder. No need for tiptoeing. The horses were already agitated, worrying they might be left behind—even though surely the turnout was the same routine every morning. I scrambled up the rungs and disappeared from view below just as the man returned, ambling toward the wide barn door.

"Where were you?" Viv asked anxiously.

"Shhh . . . ." I put my finger to my lips.

The man paused, cocking his head, listening.

I held my breath.

After a moment, he moved on to the waiting horses. *Yes, sir, that's my baby.* "Your turn, child." The stall door slid open. And the next. Vivian and I didn't move a hair while the stable hand made the trip in and out twice more, horses flanking him.

He left the chestnut for last.

I could hear all manner of fury coming from that horse's stall. Pawing with his front hooves, kicking out with his back. "Okay, okay, Red," the stable hand spoke calmly but without any of the affection he'd kissed the other horses with. "Let's be peaceable this morning. No reason to be getting into a lather. You about busted my hand yesterday pulling on me."

Bang! The horse let fly a real kick to the stall's wall that made it reverberate.

"Really? That just isn't necessary, boy." I could hear the man pull the chestnut's halter off its hook.

Bang!

"You know, brother, I've seen worse than you. You're what my mama called stuff and nonsense. Now settle. Don't be giving Mrs. Scott another reason to be rid of you. Whoa, boy. Whoa."

More pawing. *Bang!*

"Set-tle."

A little more pawing, half-hearted.

"That's it. Now we're talking." The door slid back. "Whoa. Whoa, now. Good boy." I could hear the chestnut calm and accept the halter. Then that wild horse half-dragged the poor stable hand, who had to trot himself to keep up—gimp and all.

But dang if that quarrelsome creature didn't stop at the door of the barn—stock-still—after all that fuss and hurry to get out—and turn to stare back and up toward the hayloft where Vivian and I hid.

"What in the Sam Hill," the stable hand murmured. He stroked the horse's neck. "What you looking at, boy?" But as he spoke and soothed, the horse reared slightly, landed, snorted, stamped, and trotted forward again.

That horse was trouble. And staying hidden in the hayloft was clearly going to be a circus trick to pull off, especially with that volatile chestnut around.

CHAPTER 3

Vivian bowed her head and clasped her hands. "For this we are about to receive, the Lord make us truly thankful." She missed singing in the children's choir at our old church, and she always said grace before stuffing things into her mouth like a hungry chipmunk. She peeked up at me. "Say amen, Bea."

"Amen." These days it took everything I had to utter that word.

Vivian snapped off a piece of carrot and tucked it into her biscuit as the harsh reality of the last hour washed over me. What did Daddy expect me to do? Walk up to some strange lady's front door, knock, and announce that my father had left her a little surprise? I didn't know anything about this woman except she had a bunch of fine-looking horses she clearly wasn't riding. And that she might have it out for that chestnut. What if she was some unforgiving, snooty old rich lady?

I looked down at my clothes. I wore the last dress Mama had sewn for me, big so I had room to grow as if she'd had a premonition about getting sick and leaving us—a flowered cotton in a tight pattern of rosebuds, with a sweet Peter Pan collar. The short sleeves were puffed and cuffed. Four red wooden buttons went down its front to the waist. It was a work of craft and love, but it was stained and grimy and a little frayed now at the hem. I couldn't remember when I'd last really washed it. Two weeks ago?

Putting my hand to my hair to feel the thick ribbon holding it back off my face, I wondered how dirty was that red grosgrain? My socks drooped, my shoes were scuffed and filthy. Vivian's outfit was the same—a neatly tailored dress of blue that was now wrinkled and dingy, a once bright ribbon pulling her honey-colored waves off her pretty but smudged, heart-shaped face.

I hadn't felt the full humiliation of what I had come to until that moment. And it was like falling into a well.

We . . . looked pitiful . . . like . . . like *Oliver Twist* urchins. What if this woman opened her door and was repulsed by the sight of us? She might send us to a children's home. Oh God. They might take Viv away from me.

Daddy. What were you thinking?

I shot to my feet.

"You all right, Bea?" Vivian looked up. "Did something sting you?"

"What? Yes. I mean no. I mean . . . Yes, I am all right. I just need to think a minute." I started pacing. I had always been a dutiful daughter and obeyed Daddy. But I wasn't at all certain that handing myself and Viv over to this unknown woman was so all-fired smart. I needed to know more before—if—we did that.

Coming to the other side of the hayloft, I paused at its wide-open gable. From there, I could see the beginnings of boxwood gardens and the green tin roof of a house rising over them on the other side. I should try to catch a glimpse of this Mrs. Scott. Get a sense of her circumstances. Maybe Mama's friend, Marjorie, would be out picking blooms and singing a sweet song like Mama used to, and then I would know. It would be a sign that things would be all right. That maybe I could trust these people for help.

"Viv, be a champ and stay quiet as a mouse up here for a little and let me take a look around?"

"Why?"

Agitated as I was, I couldn't help but snap, "Because."

Mistake.

Viv dug in, stubborn. "Won't. If you're going somewhere, I'm going there, too."

"Please, Vivian, just . . . you're too noisy."

"Am not!"

"Shhhhhh." I raised my hands in a gesture of see-what-I'm-saying.

"Am not," she hissed, pouting for a moment. "Why do we need to be so quiet anyway? Is it because we're in hiding until Daddy comes back to get us?"

Grateful for her assumption, I picked it up and played on it—like a pair of fiddlers toss a melody back and forth, each adding little embellishments or modulating the key—the same song, but expanded, enriched. I wasn't *starting* the fib. She couldn't later accuse me of raising false hope or promises. "If we're going to be here a few days I need to see what else I might be able to find for us to eat."

"Well, if we're supposed to be stealthy," Vivian said, "you'll be needing a lookout."

"For what?"

"For the old man." Vivian pointed out the hayloft's other door.

The stable hand was heading back.

"Viv! Get back from the opening. Quick." We receded into the loft's shadows.

We had to stay there for a long time as the man

mucked out seven stalls, singing or humming the whole time a song I'd heard on the radio.

I had nothing but shadows . . .

Schwoop. That sound was his scooping up a pitchfork full of manure out of the stall's sawdust bedding.

Then one morning you passed . . .

Thunk. He dumped the dung into a wheelbarrow.

All my worry blew away . . .

Schwoop. Thunk.

Just . . .

He paused his song and slowly, with a loud grunt, tilted and moved the wheelbarrow to the next stall as it squeaked loudly. He wasn't doing a full mucking and stripping the stalls, thank God. Just picking up piles from the night. Five, ten minutes a stall maybe. Still, that math meant we were probably in for a forty-minute wait or so. I motioned for Vivian to nestle into the hay—and for pity's sake do it quietly.

Schwoop. Thunk.

Just direct your feet . . .

Schwoop. Thunk.

On the sun-ny side of the street . . .

The man might be old and beaten up and slow moving, but he obviously had a musical and hopeful soul. I knew the song—all about love compensating for bad luck and life sorrows. It was one of many written recently trying to encourage a positive attitude in us despite the Great Depression. I didn't hear any doubt or scoffing at the lyrics as the stable hand sang them. Clearly, he was an optimist.

So, a potential fool.

I sucked in a sharp breath, shocked that I would think that way. But I was considering all manner of new thoughts, right disrespectful ones, as of this morning.

When he was finally done and gone, poor Vivian looked like she might explode from needing to go herself.

"Come on, Viv," I pulled her to her feet. "We can pee in the stall shavings."

There was no way of keeping her in the stable at that point, so I took Viv with me, figuring I might luck into a way of amusing her in the boxwood gardens. They seemed to be planted in a maze, maybe a century old they were so big. They rose tall and thick, throwing shadows along a lawn that was ankle deep. Been awhile since its grass had been mown. Hand in hand, Vivian and I scurried toward the first hedge wall of boxwood.

"Ooh, look at all the clover in the grass!" Viv exclaimed as we traipsed through its delicate white blossoms. "Can we pick some and make a chain?" she warbled.

"Maybe later, Viv, we need to get to the cover of the boxwood," I urged her forward.

We reached the entrance break in the boxwood and were enveloped in a magical, dark-green coolness. Once upon a long time ago, someone had laid out meticulously symmetrical lines of bushes. Now grown tall, the dirt paths between them led to little secret enclaves, decorated with statues of nymphs, flowerbeds of peonies, lilies, and iris, falling all over one another in crowds of colors—red, orange, and blue.

The garden overflowed with weeds and calf-high dandelions too, but somehow, that only heightened my wonderment, my sense of discovering another world, like in one of my favorite books, *The Secret Garden*. For the first time in . . . in . . . I don't know when, I felt total enchantment.

We turned again and again, and came to its center, a little lily pond, rimmed with fieldstones. Just like the one Mama had made at home in our garden. Lying beside it was a mason jar filled with oatmeal flakes.

Viv grabbed it up. "There must be koi fish!"

Just like at home.

"Can I? Can I?"

I nodded.

Sure enough, the instant Viv scattered a little oatmeal on the water, bright-orange fish rose to the surface, their wide mouths opening and shutting greedily.

Oatmeal. I almost drooled over something I

used to hate. I could take some of those flakes, mix in some powdered milk, and boil it with water to make us what Mama would call a rib-sticking meal.

"Oh, Bea," Vivian whispered, "look at them. There's one that's all spots. Ooh, and look how pretty the black-and-orange one is!"

Seeing those whiskery fish gobble their fill of oatmeal, all I could wonder on was what they would taste like fried up.

No matter what, no matter how bad it gets, we never steal, little one. I heard Mama's voice when she took Viv and me back to the five and dime after we'd made off with two lollipops we couldn't pay for. She'd made us give them back and apologize. The grocer had offered to let us have them anyway. But Mama had refused.

I felt my face turn the same crimson it had that day. I'd leave the lady-of-the-manor's pet goldfish alone. "Viv, can you stay here for a few minutes and watch the fish?"

She looked up from her crouch by the pond, considering. She nodded solemnly.

"Just slide between two bushes if someone comes. They're so full, you'll disappear."

She nodded again.

I went to see what person was lucky enough to live here.

CHAPTER 4

Going back to the boxwood garden's entrance, I assessed the front of the house and its outbuildings scattered behind. The original part of the house was relatively small, made of field-stone, three big windows, one per room across its second floor, one window on either side of the front door and its wide, whitewashed portico. It seemed to have two different, larger clapboard additions, likely added as each generation of the family birthed its children and had good years of farming. Beside it, three ancient oaks stood sentry, lending shade.

Hearing what had to be a screen door slam—not that heavy, so not that loud—I still startled. The sound cut across those open fields! Viv and I really had to be careful. I heard a male voice. Different from the stable hand's. Deeper. A female one answering. Another slam of the door. They were coming out back somewhere. I sprinted to a tree, using it as a shield as if playing hide-and-seek. Another and then another to work my way toward the sound, skirting the house's perimeter. I noticed its clapboard wings were in sore need of some new paint.

I came to a tool shed on the other side, realizing too late that I was dangerously close to two people hanging laundry on the clothesline to dry. I skittered inside it, careful to not knock any of the scythes and clippers and wrenches and mallets dangling from hooks on its walls. I peeped out through its window.

Slender, posture perfect, the lady moved with a quick, easy grace that would make her seem younger than her full-on gray hair suggested. She wore it shorn in a bob, glasses on her head. She'd tied a colorful short scarf at her throat, but the rest of her outfit was pure sensible. Her blouse was loose, sleeves rolled up, tucked into blousy jodhpurs, topped with green wellies. Mrs. Scott—had to be.

She struggled a bit with getting the clothespins securely fastened to the sheets. I recognized what that fumbling meant from watching my father—she was new to the chore of washing clothes and getting them on the line. Which suggested she was used to having a maid, who clearly was no longer coming to work. And judging from the overgrown lawn and weeds, no more gardener, either.

I chewed on that information. That would mean Mrs. Scott was having to economize, didn't have the money to pay those workers. Would the lady really be of a mind to afford handouts to unknown children?

This man's identity was a bit of a puzzlement. He looked to be a good thirty years younger than she was, Black, tall, strong-looking, but uncertain in his movements. He just stood, holding the other end of the sheet as she worked the pins down it. And then waited, arms at his side, until she reached into the basket for the next sheet, asking him to take the other end. I watched him grope the edge of the basket and then find the linen. Lift and shake, droplets spraying them both, and then onto the line.

I couldn't hear through the window glass, so when the basket was empty and she leaned over to pick it up, I crept to the open door to catch whatever was said next. All I heard was his baritone reassurance, "I'm all right, ma'am. The sun is bright out here, so I can see shapes clear enough." He made his way to the back door carefully, took one step at a time, and entered the house.

Mrs. Scott followed, but she abruptly paused in her own loping stride, her attention caught by something.

In the distance came a bone-chilling baying and howling. High and low, growing louder by the second. A pack of dogs all whipped up about something.

Basket on one hip, her hand on the other, Mrs.

Scott stamped one of her wellies. "Oafs. It's off season!" Then she shouted, to no one I could see, "Stay out of my corn, you thoughtless fools."

Dropping the basket she hurried—moving right spritely for a grande dame, I must say—calling, "Malachi! We need to get to the cornfields to stop riders from jumping my fences and trampling the corn shoots. In case the fox comes this way. Those nitwits could ruin the whole crop if they yahoo through. Fools." The door slammed behind her.

I can't say I was feeling confident about Mrs. Scott. The woman clearly had a temper.

Slowly I made my way back to Viv, trying to muddle out what to do given what I'd just witnessed. Mrs. Scott had clearly fallen on some hard times herself. I'd seen no sign of the daughter Marjorie either, the lady who'd been Mama's college roommate. Mama might have thought the women had good hearts—and she'd had a remarkable sixth sense about people—but money worries do things to people.

Look what it had done to Daddy.

How long had it been since Mama had seen the Scotts, anyway? I didn't recollect hearing anything about them before. Mama got married pretty much straight out of college and had me a little over a year later—so maybe fifteen years since she had last been here? Could it have been that long? Would Mrs. Scott even remember who Mama was?

Working my way through the boxwood, I took several dead-end turns, discovering new little alcoves with statues or birdbaths, before finally finding the path leading directly to the lily pond. I called out in a forced whisper, "It's me," as I entered the maze's inner circle.

"Lookee!" Viv was sitting cross-legged, her skirt pulled to be as full as possible over her knees. Grinning, she pointed to her lap. "Peepers!"

She'd filled her skirt with tiny frogs, no bigger than a man's thumb—the ones who make such a sweet chorus at night in the spring and early summer. I flopped down beside her and one of the delicate frogs hopped onto my arm, damp, jade green, winking.

"Bea?" Vivian began.

"Hmm?"

"When Daddy comes back to get us, if he doesn't already have a job, maybe he could get one here. I like this place."

It took all manner of self-control to not cry. How could I tell Viv that Daddy had just up and left? And that she better not like this place too much. Or any place.

Rolling onto my stomach, I stared at dandelion weeds so she couldn't see my expression. Well, at least there was part of our dinner. I sat up and started yanking. I'd learned the weeds were edible from one of our neighbors in that street of rattle-trap bungalows Daddy moved us to down by the James River wharves after we lost our house.

Gnats circled my head, like the swarms of mos-quitoes that had plagued us there. I didn't know it for sure, but I swear a bite from one of those bloodsuckers is what killed Mama with fever. To save money, the city had stopped spraying for mosquitoes, just like they'd cut off streetlamps, laid off bus drivers, and closed kindergartens. A whole lot of people in that neighborhood got sick that summer.

"Play with me!" Vivian pounced, knocking me over.

"Get off!" I rolled her away.

"Come on, Bea. Leapfrog!"

Giggling, Vivian hopped once, twice, three times over me before I caught her by the ankle. "Stop it," I hissed. "How about you help me instead of bedeviling me?"

Vivian kneeled. "Sorry, Bea." She yanked up a few, then whimpered, "Need some water."

I sighed. That child had terrible trouble sticking to a task. But we'd pulled more greens than we could eat anyway. And tearing them up had burned off some of my fury. I gathered the dandelions into my arms. "There's sure to be a water spicket around the stable. Let's go."

Somehow, we came out of a different part of that garden, farther from the house, facing an orchard. Both our faces lit up. "Peaches!" Viv gasped, bolting for the trees.

"Only a couple, Viv," I cautioned. But she

had already reached the first branches, plucked a peach, and taken a huge bite.

"Oh, it's lovely," she cried. "Try one."

I touched one of those beautiful, fuzzy orbs of pink-orange and it detached, dropping to my hand. It was that ripe. Dozens and dozens of peaches hung above me, jewels, ready. In that one tree alone. If Mrs. Scott didn't harvest them soon, they might go bad. Which would be an unspeakable waste. Did she not have any pickers?

As I plucked another, I heard in the distance that *yip-yip-yipping* of hounds. And within moments a red fox trotted across the hayfields, heading right for us. Moving apace, but not seeming overly concerned about the dogs hunting him. Suddenly, he leaped into the air beside a bush-sized thistle, a gorgeous streak of crimson vaulting and plunging into the green. A furious spray of debris followed. He was digging up something. Then the grasses parted, and he emerged. Noticing us, he stopped, sat, ears twitching.

After a moment of our staring at each other, he decided we were harmless and trotted nearer and nearer—he sure was a bodacious creature. He got to within a few yards before he veered toward a stone wall rimming the orchard. Up and over and then gone. But I'd seen that egg in his mouth.

A quail's nest was by that thistle. Oh, we were going to have a feast for dinner!

CHAPTER 5

"You know," Viv drew out the two words to make sure I was listening.

I looked up.

"There are boys making money by sitting in trees. I saw a photograph of one in a newspaper floating around in that cargo car we were riding on the way here. A boy just a little older than I am had climbed straight to the top of a big ole pine tree and sat there. For days and days and days. People were dropping donations in a coin box he'd left at the bottom of the tree. And a Norfolk hardware owner was going to pay him a whole ten cents to hold up a sign about his store if he lasted a week."

She skipped over to a nearby maple, jumped to catch a low limb, and swung her legs up on it. "I told Daddy I could earn money for us that way. I am an excellent tree climber."

"Mm-hmm," I murmured, and carefully turned over the little quail eggs I was frying in the iron skillet we carried with us. Daddy had left the satchel of cooking necessities—the fry pan, a bowl, a stewpot, a saltshaker now empty, and two wooden spoons to stir and flip things. I worried how he might fend for himself, followed by a terrible thought that cold food would serve him right for leaving us.

Letting her arms dangle, Vivian hung upside down by her knees as she said, "How do you suppose a tree-sitter eats . . . or . . . takes care of his business?"

"Now there's something to ponder." I pulled

the eggs off my little fire and blew on them to cool. "Throw some dirt on that fire, Viv, to put it out."

She flipped herself down as deft as any circus acrobat and kicked sod onto the flames.

We were on the edge of a pasture, far from the house and sheds to avoid accidentally setting something on fire. Daddy had taught me that much in our wanderings. But we were out in the open, and I worried about being spotted. So we headed back to the stable. It took every ounce of manners Mama had talked into me to keep myself from sticking my face into that pan to slurp up those eggs as I walked.

Back up in the hayloft I laid out the eggs, the dandelion greens I'd sautéed to get the bite out of their taste, and the cut-up peaches. Honestly, it was the prettiest and biggest meal we'd had in days. Didn't matter the eggs were slightly scorched.

We clinked our forks. "Thank you, Mr. Fox," I said.

Maybe we could survive here for a while. It sure was easier than scavenging food on city streets.

~

We sat munching, watching the sun slide behind not-too-distant low mountains, turning them a gorgeous ridge of purple-blue, backlit by halos of enormous sunrays. Twilight was different in this corner of Virginia. Back home in the Tidewater, the earth was mostly flat, and the sun setting was a gentle, pink splash across quiet marshes.

Here the sun disappeared fast behind those hills, so the landscape around us went dark quickly, shadows rolling out in long carpets of mystery. Clouds took their time turning from light-infused golden pink to a rosy blush to a rich ruby to a dense purple. Only then did they give way to a lapis gray and disappear from view, their color seeping into the blackening sky.

Beautiful but fierce. Even a little menacing if you had a fearful heart or believed in premonitions.

"Think Daddy will be back for us tomorrow?" Vivian asked.

I hesitated. Daddy had faded into the unknown

like those clouds into the inky night. But I couldn't say that—not tonight. Vivian needed to sleep. Still, my answer couldn't be baloney. If I said something as if it were for certain—even if just a little fib to soothe her through a hard moment—and then it didn't happen, Vivian would spend the next day discombobulated, murmuring, "But you said . . . ."

You have to mean what you say with a child. Adults seem to forget that.

"I hope so," I finally answered. That was true enough.

Her lower lip quivered.

"Finish your dandelions, Viv."

"Don't want them."

I didn't either. Bitter-tasting weeds pulled up out of neglected flowerbeds while I crouched, afraid of being spotted? Not exactly what I wanted for my supper. "You need them. Don't argue. Eat up."

"Don't have to be mean about it," she grumbled, a tear crystalizing in the corner of her eye.

I sighed. "You can have another peach if you eat all those."

Brightening instantly, Vivian crammed a fistful

of the limp dark leaves into her mouth and grinned as she chomped, very pleased with herself.

Boy, did I fall for that. I couldn't help laughing, though. Knowing she hated the fuzz, I peeled off the peach's skin with the penknife I'd saved from the day the bank made us put all our belongings out for people to bid on at the auction of our home to pay off Daddy's debts. (Someone had had to be practical that awful day.)

I handed Vivian a slice as I popped a hunk into my own mouth and let the sweetness melt on my tongue.

"Oh, look!" Vivian stopped licking peach juice off her fingertips to point toward the outside gloom. "Fireflies!"

Little flecks of light were bubbling up from the ground and drifting into the air.

"Can we go catch some? There must be a jar in the stable somewhere. We can fill it with grass and poke holes in the lid, and they can be like a fairy lantern for us tonight!"

Vivian started to scramble to her feet. "Pretty please?"

I grabbed her hand to hold her in place. I'd witnessed her chase fireflies before, laughing and leaping as the little insects blinked on and off, swerving about, instinctively evading our grasp. Viv's joy was *loud*. "Better not call attention to ourselves, honey. Not . . . not tonight anyway."

She slumped, pouting. But she took my arm, lifted it up and over her shoulders, and snuggled in beside me. The fireflies wafted higher, tiny beacons of incandescent life, bobbing as they floated higher and higher into the dark trees.

"What makes them do that?" Viv murmured.

"No idea. They are gorgeous, though, aren't they? They only do it for a couple of weeks and then we won't see them again until next June."

The fireflies began to settle into the treetops, winking and sparkling there, like a small, flickering Milky Way of earthly stars.

"That's sad," Vivian murmured, "to be so beautiful and then just disappear. Why do they go away for a whole year?"

"I don't know."

"Where do they go?"

“I don’t know.”

We both fell silent for a few moments, watching the dance of tiny twinkles. Then I speculated, “Maybe there is a queen—like bees have—who tells them what to do and when.”

“Oh. Maybe.” Vivian gave me a mischievous grin. “Like a bossy boss?”

Catching her insinuation, I bristled, itching to shout: *You try being in charge of keeping us fed, of having to be a mother to a squirt like you. And now a father, too! See if you wouldn’t be a mite bossy!* But Vivian yawned, snuggling in closer, like we both used to with Mama when she spun one of her bedtime stories for us.

It was hard to be annoyed with my rowdy little sister when she was being sweet. I softened. “Or maybe,” I said, “they have a little princess. Maybe a little princess named—”

“Named Viv-Viv-Viv!”

I laughed. “Yes, a little princess named Viv-Viv-Viv.”

“Tell!”

After Mama died, I’d started telling stories

to make us forget we were hungry at bedtime. "Well . . . once upon a long time ago, Viv was a mere insect. A beautiful one—"

"Of course, she is, given her name!" Vivian prompted.

"To be sure, a very beautiful one. But Viv-Viv-Viv couldn't seem to fly, even though she had wings. And she couldn't light up with happiness, even though the green grass and the blue sky touched her heart. It was as if she couldn't trust them or herself. As if she were afraid that if she admitted joy, they'd vanish."

Vivian curled up and laid her head on my knee.

"But she was a very stubborn little bug." I stroked my sister's sun-colored hair and lowered my voice to lullaby quiet. "So, one day, Viv-Viv-Viv climbed the mountain to speak to Mother Nature. No one else would have been so brave . . . or so impertinent. At first Mother Nature was put out by"—I paused for emphasis—"her moxie!" referencing Vivian's favorite soft drink. Its name had become slang for nerve, since its gentian root was supposed to perk up even the slowest slug of a person. Its effect on Vivian had been a tad terrifying.

Vivian giggled.

Fleetingly, I wondered how long it had been since we'd had a sip of that tangy soda pop. I pushed myself back to the story. "Mother Nature threatened to squish the brash little bug with a lightning bolt for not respecting her elders, but Viv-Viv-Viv thought quickly and said, 'Oh, Mother Nature, the wisest and prettiest goddess of them all. If, in your infinite kindness, you will let me fly, I will find a way to thank you with each flutter so the whole world and all the silly humans in it will marvel at your great artistry.'

"That was very clever of Viv-Viv-Viv, because truth be known, Mother Nature does have a bit of a prideful soul. 'Why,' the deity responded, 'that sounds a marvelous idea, little bug.' Mother Nature kissed Viv-Viv-Viv on the head, like this." Gently, I kissed Vivian's short curls. "And with that, Viv-Viv-Viv suddenly felt herself glowing with happiness and hope, and, lo and behold, her whole body lit up like . . ."

Vivian's breath was suddenly slow and sing-songy. She was asleep.

". . . like a little drop of starlight," I whispered.

I pulled Vivian's sweater up over her, leaned against a hayloft beam, and, watching the fireflies, refused to think about Daddy or what would happen tomorrow. Today had been better than it might have been—all things considered. I'd fed my little sister and kept a new fear from giving her nightmares. That's all a body could do these days. One day, one meal at a time.

But when my heart started aching all the same, and the feeling of being an abandoned, thrown-away thing choked me, I made myself count the fireflies. *One—don't think. Two—don't think.* Somewhere around three-hundred-something I must have drifted off.

CHAPTER 6

Six days passed with our hiding safely, like mice, in the hayloft. At night, Vivian insisted on pulling her Ouija board out from her little suitcase and asking it when Daddy would find a job. What it would be. When he'd be back for us. Where we would live then.

I did the best I could to push its teardrop planchette toward letters that would spell out *everything will be fine.* I could feel her fingers trying just as hard to will it toward *soon* and *something wonderful* and *in a lovely house with window boxes filled with geraniums*. I know that stupid talking board was all the rage, had been popular ever since spiritualists in the last century had claimed to talk to the dead through it. But the thing gave me the creeps.

Daddy had let Vivian keep the Ouija because she was convinced Mama might talk to us through it. As if that were a good idea. I was coming to realize Daddy just wasn't any good at the hard part of parenting.

Mrs. Scott didn't come near the barn—even though whenever I spotted her, she was in her jodhpurs like she was going out for a hack. And the old stable hand, as careful and attentive as he was to the horses, seemed a mite oblivious to other things. He kept leaving his lunch in the tack room and not coming back for it. How absentminded could you get? Bits of cheese and hunks of bread wrapped up in brown paper.

I'd reckoned we had to eat them—it would just attract mice if we didn't.

But this morning as he came in through the early mist singing "There's a Rainbow Round My

Shoulder," he told the horses something guaranteed to make our life as hideaways even harder.

"Good morning, you old beauty," he greeted the mare who always nickered when she spotted him. "I must ask your patience tomorrow, ma'am. I'm going to keep you in your stalls until twilight instead of letting you out in the morning. Switching you from day to night turnout to save y'all from the flies and broiling sun. Mrs. Scott's plumb forgotten about the summer swelter, she's so worried about other things. But I'm seeing how hot and riled y'all are getting out in the fields in the heat. So, I'm not waiting for her to tell me to do the flip. But that means you have to stay in when you're expecting to go out. I'll babysit y'all through the change-over. But you talk to everyone for me, all right? That chestnut is gonna have a fit about it. Let's hope he don't try to kick me again."

The stable hand moved on to the bays. "I'm going to be needing lots of hay, ain't I, fellas, to distract you until it's time to turn out. Have to crawl up that ladder a couple times, I 'spect. Me and my old bones. Yup. All day. Back and forth to the hayloft. Back and forth."

Then he whistled his way down to the feed room.

The stable hand would be in the barn the whole day? Coming into the loft for hay? What would we do? My mind whirled.

But we didn't even make it to that crisis. Disaster came in the night.

At first it was just a rustling. Then a moaning. *Thump!*

I jolted upright from the hay. I swear the hair on my head about stood straight up, too, with my thinking maybe Vivian had actually conjured up some ghost with that darn Ouija board of hers.

Moonlight spilled into the hayloft, but not bright enough that I could see into the corners. What was in them and their abyss of shadows? I bit my lip to keep from crying out: "Go away!" Instead, I threw a fistful of hay toward nothing.

Thump! I jumped.

More moaning. I covered my ears in fear.

Bang! The floorboards quaked.

BANG! They shook even more.

Trembling, I made myself stand and creep toward the ladder. Something was below.

BANG! Anguished murmuring, thrashing.

The horses started pacing and nickering anxiously. Something was spooking them.

I glanced back to Viv. How could she sleep through this? Was I just dreaming it all?

BANG!

Awful, racked moaning.

And then a desperate neighing.

That's when I knew. It was a horse. In pain.

I half-slid down the ladder and fell to my knees in my hurry.

The mare whinnied.

"Shhh-shhh," I begged, and groped my way down the aisle in the gloom.

It wasn't either of the bays. The roan snorted, alarmed at my appearance out of nowhere, but he was fine, the dappled-grays frightened but not contorting.

BANG! Another tortured neigh.

It was the chestnut.

Of course it had to be him. A horse that might kill a child with his kick on a good day.

BANG!

I looked through the iron grating of his stall. He was down on his side, rolling, snorting, biting at his belly, frantic. *BANG!* His back hooves thrust out in agony, striking the wall.

I had never seen it before. But I knew what was wrong. He was colicking.

Mama had told me about it once so I would recognize it in Dandy and find her as fast as possible if it happened. Horses' innards were ridiculously delicate, she'd said, with seventy feet of intestines snaked up inside their torso. Any blockage, any twist in those bowels could kill them because they can't vomit. They don't even burp.

The remedy? Getting a horse to poop. And that required him being on his feet, walking.

BANG! The chestnut writhed. The more he wrenched around, the greater danger of getting a complete and deadly twist in his intestines.

He wasn't going to make it until morning. And

he was making so much noise as he fought the pain, if her windows were open to the night air for a cooling breeze, Mrs. Scott was bound to hear the commotion.

Instinct got the better of my common sense. I pushed back the stall door.

BANG! The chestnut looked up at me with wild, suffering eyes.

BANG! He rolled and neighed—a long, tormented, heart-wrenching cry.

I needed to get him up. Fast. How the heck was I going to do that? It's not like I could pull him to his feet. He weighed twelve hundred pounds at least. And I couldn't offer him a treat. Food would only make matters worse.

"Whoa, boy." I crouched and stroked his neck and used the name I'd heard the stable hand call him, "Whoa, Red."

The chestnut flailed and whipped his head around to bite me, his teeth bared. I fell back on my butt.

BANG!

He thrashed around more, snorting, whinnying so loud his ribs shook with the sound, kicking up his stall shavings in the distraught twisting. But he kept those huge eyes, wide in fear, on me. No matter how much he was fighting it, he was desperate for help. I could see it.

"All right, brother," again I used the stable hand's names. "I get it. I know. I know. I feel that way a lot too these days." I reached out again, slowly, to touch his neck.

This time he calmed a little.

"That's it, Red. That's it." I kept stroking. His contorting slowed.

I took another chance, one I'd yell at Viv for if I ever caught her doing it with a horse this combative—I leaned over to blow, gently, into his huge nostril. If he bit at me again, he could take a hunk of my face. But it's how horses greet one another or show affection, nose to nose, breathing a bit of their soul into the other. It was the only thing I could think of to get him to trust me—fast.

The chestnut's nostrils twitched.

I did it again. "Let me help you." I stroked his neck. "It's okay, brother. Set-tle. Set-tle. Good. Good boy."

The chestnut eased down to a pained snorting, and I pulled his halter off its hook and slipped it over his head. He twitched, rolling his eyes, their white showing in his misery. But he didn't kick.

I stood up and stepped back to give him room and get me out of danger. Horses lifting themselves to their hooves can be an almost violent surge. "You've got to get up, Red. Up. Get up, brother. Stand."

He struggled, struggled, moaned, struggled, but then rose, shaking himself, wobbly on those long legs. But almost immediately he started to buckle.

"No, no, boy. We've got to walk." I snapped the lead line on him quick, stepped into the aisle, and tugged a little.

His front legs started to bend at his knee. The first sign of a horse going down.

"No, fella, no," I held my hand out to trick him into thinking I had a treat. "Walk on, boy,"

I urged him. "Walk on. Sometimes you just gotta walk on, brother, no matter how bad you feel." I snapped the line a little, to wake him out of his pain. He jerked his head back and stamped in protest. But he moved.

"That's it. Good boy. Walk on."

His head hanging, the chestnut followed. *Clop . . . clop . . . clop . . . clop.* He stopped. Whipped his head back to bite at his belly, as if he could yank the ache out of himself. I winced, seeing he'd nipped himself raw on his side.

"Come on. That's it."

We got out of the barn, but he lowered his head to the grass, instinctively wanting to graze on the tender green.

I pulled on him. "No, no, Red. We've got to walk."

I'd have to walk him around the ring, where there was nothing but sand. Thankfully, the stars and moonlight were bright so I could see the footing. Slowly, we walked along the fence line.

First full circle. He was staggering, balking, but he followed.

Second circle. Fourth. Tenth. Had we been doing this an hour?

He stopped again, bowed, dropped to his knees, and flopped to his side to roll and roll and roll, his whickering more like a child's whimper now.

I grabbed him by the halter and yanked. "Not now, boy. You can do this. You have to. Or you'll die." I realized I was crying. What an idiot. What did I care about this horse? He wasn't mine and he clearly had a questionable personality. But tears were misting my vision, making my hands slippery. I just couldn't watch something else die. I just couldn't. "Please, boy. Get up. Please don't die. Please. GET. UP!"

And—in a stubborn, last ditch struggle that made me cry all the more—the chestnut stumbled to his feet, his snorting weak, halting, fading.

Twentieth circle.

The moon began to sink in the sky.

Thirtieth.

I could barely walk anymore. One foot. Next foot. One foot. Next. *Clop. Clop. Clop. Clop.*

And then, just as I was about to fall down in

defeat and exhaustion, and the dark trees in the distance glowed red, backlit with the rising sun, he stopped. Wouldn't budge. Lifted his tail and . . . *plop. Plop . . . plop, plop.*

Manure. Salvation.

He sighed and shook his mane.

I threw my arms around his neck. "Good boy!"

The chestnut stamped but rested his head on my shoulder for just a moment before starting to jog and weave, his natural, standoffish defiance coming over him again. But he nudged me with his lowered head, once, as if in thanks. I knew it, even though it was rough enough to make me stagger. "Let's get you back to the stall," I murmured, patting him. "Before someone sees us."

I turned us toward the gate.

And there, in the dawn's shadows, stood Mrs. Scott.

CHAPTER 7

My mouth opened. Shut. I looked from side to side, but all there was to hide behind were some rail jumps. Oh God. I closed my eyes and willed myself to just evaporate. As if that were possible.

Mrs. Scott didn't speak.

I waited, absolutely paralyzed. What felt about a week's worth of time passed, the sun climbing, pouring pink light into the ring, slowly lighting up Mrs. Scott's moon-pale face. Thin with startingly pronounced high cheekbones, big wide-set eyes, graying and unfashionable, unplucked brows. No smile.

Finally, the chestnut lowered his head to my backside and knocked me from behind. I staggered forward. Did it again, so hard I nearly fell to my knees.

"Best walk forward, young lady. Before he hurts you."

Like the idiot I had become, I shook my head. I didn't want to get near her—then she'd see me. As I said, I'd left my brain in the barn.

"Come, come, girl. I can tell you're not stupid. I think you might have just saved that horse from a colic. Am I right?"

Slowly, I nodded.

He knocked me again.

"That chestnut can be dangerous when impatient. Walk on." Her voice was calm, smooth, not mean. But clearly she brooked no foolishness or fear.

I obeyed. One foot in front of the other, I started to cross the ring toward her. But oh, how my heart pounded. I thought my chest would explode.

Still no smile.

Could I dart past her, grab Vivian, and run? How agile was this lady?

Then I heard whistling, singing. *I've got rhythm, I got music, I got my gal, who could ask for anything more.* The stable hand appeared. Halted. "Why good morning, ma'am," he greeted Mrs. Scott with the same jolly friendliness he talked to the horses. "It's mighty good to see you down here. I was just thinking that—" He broke off, spotting me.

"Good day, Ralph." She kept her gaze on me as she asked him, "This one of your grandchildren?"

He paused. "Well, now, ma'am, I was going to tell you—"

"Please don't be spinning me one of your tales, Ralph. Is this girl kin to you?"

"No, ma'am."

"You been hiding a drifter again?"

A long pause. "Well now, ma'am," he began the same way, "I just noticed the other day what I thought might be two little girls out in the fields, and they seemed—"

"Two?" At this, Mrs. Scott turned around to

look at Ralph. “Two? Any parents?”

The stable hand shook his head.

He knew? Recognition flooded me—the bits of food left in the tack room. The loud talk yesterday about having to go up in the loft. I felt tears well up again—he was kind.

But what about her?

Gazing at me, Mrs. Scott pursed her lips. Then she gestured toward me and the horse. “The girl certainly has horse sense. Although it’s hard to see right now.” She assessed me for another moment. The chestnut knocked me again, stamped, pawed the sand.

“Ralph, take that beast from her before he hurts her. He was colicking, but she got him to pass manure. Give him a dose of mineral oil and then put him in the sick paddock. You’ll need to keep an eye on him today, I’m afraid. And he’ll need mash tonight. Troublesome thing.”

“Yes, ma’am.” He came and took the chestnut from me. He winked as I handed him the lead line and whispered, “Do exactly as she says, child, and you have a fighting chance.”

Still speechless, I nodded.

"Been walking that fool horse all night?" Mrs. Scott asked as Ralph led the chestnut, all full of himself now, past her and entered the stable.

I nodded.

"You must be hungry."

I nodded.

"Where's the other girl?"

We heard a scrambling at the barn's open loft and looked up to see a flash of Vivian diving back inside to the hay. She'd clearly been watching the whole exchange.

Did I see a glimmer of amusement on Mrs. Scott's face? "Your sister?"

I nodded.

"Get her and come to the kitchen. I'll give you a decent breakfast. No dawdling now. I have things to do today. Be up to the house in five minutes."

Turning on her heel, she strode toward her house, muttering about having to "call the sheriff now, as if I have time for that."

"What's she like?" Vivian whispered, as trembling, holding her by the hand, I steered us to the house.

"Scary."

Vivian's amber eyes grew big. "How scary?"

"Don't know yet. But . . . like a school headmistress. So, mind your manners."

Mrs. Scott had given us five minutes. I could tell she meant it. So, I'd only been able to dust the hay off our clothes and run a comb through our hair. I started to pull Daddy's note from its hiding place but thought better of it. I needed to know more about this woman before revealing our daddy expected her to take us on.

As we walked across the lawn, my mind bucked with a mess of feelings—fear, fury at Daddy, hurt, humiliation, hope, hunger, so much hunger. *A decent breakfast.* As we neared the back door, I caught the heavenly smell of biscuits, pulled fresh from the oven and, oh my, was that—

"Bacon!" Vivian darted ahead of me.

"Viv!"

But she was already at the back door, knocking. I ran to catch up.

Mrs. Scott swung the screen door open and looked down at Vivian. "You are the sister, I presume."

Vivian's mouth popped open.

"Don't catch flies, young lady."

Vivian shut her mouth, pressing her lips together.

"You have a name?"

"Y-yes, ma'am."

Mrs. Scott waited, raising an eyebrow.

"It's Vivian," I said, putting my hands on my little sister's shoulders and squeezing to reassure her.

"And yours?"

"Beatrice."

She nodded. "Come in then, Beatrice and Vivian. I am Mrs. Scott." She gestured to a man standing by a stove, cooking the bacon, the man I'd seen before with the laundry. "This is Malachi."

"Morning," he said, looking over our heads into air at first until we murmured "morning" in reply. Only then did his gaze come down to our level. He smiled. It felt reassuring and protective somehow, even though I could tell his eyes didn't really truly completely focus on us. I wondered what had happened to him, or if he'd always had trouble seeing.

"Sit." Mrs. Scott put a china bowl full of biscuits and a dish of soft butter on the table and then walked to the ice box. I had to catch Vivian's hand as it shot out to grab a biscuit. "Wait till we're told," I whispered.

Her back was toward us, but I'm pretty sure Mrs. Scott nodded slightly hearing me as she poured us two glasses of milk.

Cold, real milk.

Then Malachi put a plate heaped with bacon and scrambled eggs in front of each of us. I about drooled.

"I'll be feeding the hens now, ma'am," he said.

"Thank you, Malachi." Mrs. Scott passed us the biscuits, told us to eat, and watched him leave, running his hand along the wall as he went. She didn't turn back to us until he was out the door safely and crossing the yard, his hand running along the clothesline as he walked.

I had to force myself to not inhale my food

while Vivian showed no such hesitation.

Mrs. Scott watched us eat, sipping tea from a china teacup.

Somewhere a clock ticked loudly.

When I'd finished and Vivian was nibbling on a third biscuit, Mrs. Scott put her teacup down. "Right. So. You know horses?"

"Yes, ma'am."

"How?"

"I had a pony. And Mama rode. Before the crash."

Mrs. Scott mulled that over a bit. "Where is your mama now?"

"In heaven," Vivian murmured through a mouthful of biscuit.

"Your father?"

"Looking for work," Vivian answered again before I could. "He'll come for us when he finds it," she added with conviction before putting the last of her biscuit into her mouth.

"And he left you in my stable, expecting you to hide there until he came back?" Once again there was nothing mean in Mrs. Scott's tone, just matter-of-fact bluntness. But it knifed me.

"Yes, ma'am," I managed to get out. Without thinking, I put my hand on Viv's.

Mrs. Scott noted it. "I am beholden to you, young lady, for saving the chestnut, or at the very least saving me from an expensive visit from the vet. But I need to call the sheriff now."

"But—"

She held up her hand. "You are not in trouble. You have done nothing wrong. But I need to tell him your father a—"

I knew the word she was about to use was *abandoned* and I flinched.

Her voice softened. A little. "I need to tell the sheriff that your father can't care for you right now. The sheriff is a good man. He will know what is best for—"

I was shaking my head so violently she stopped talking. My hand tightened on Vivian's.

Mrs. Scott stood, walked toward the window over the kitchen sink. She seemed to have a habit of talking aloud to herself as she thought. "I am just barely keeping us afloat as it is," she murmured.

I watched her back—*please, please don't call the sheriff*—and noticed a bowl of peaches on the counter near the sink.

Peaches! "Mrs. Scott," I said, the words tumbling over themselves, "I noticed that you have a lovely orchard of peaches."

She turned around, clearly surprised by my shift in topic.

"They look mighty ripe. Like . . . like they need picking . . . right fast."

"Yes," she answered. "I was actually heading out there at dawn to start picking them myself when I spotted you."

My mouth popped open a bit and I snapped it shut. "No offense, ma'am. But that's an awful lot for one body to pick."

She looked to the backyard, clearly considering Malachi.

"Or just two." I stopped myself from adding, especially one who clearly didn't see very well.

Her gaze returned to me, and I thought I detected the slightest smile again on that porcelain-still face.

I had a hunch. "Pickers coming?" I asked. We'd seen some migrant workers camped along the road, all their belongings tied to the back of their old pickup. A mattress, tenting, a rocking chair, pots and pans dangling on its side. But I figured if she was hiring, some would already be in the orchard working.

Crossing her arms, Mrs. Scott leaned her backside against the sink. "I'm afraid I am unable to pay crop pickers this year."

Bingo! Thought so.

"I'm a good worker, Mrs. Scott," I burbled. "And Vivian—she can help, too. She's quite the tree climber."

Vivian brightened. "I sure am. I was telling Bea that I could be a tree-sitter and—"

I nudged her to quiet, then held my breath, chewing on my lower lip.

Mrs. Scott eyed me. There was that clock ticking again—like judgment pacing. "All right, then." She stood up and strode back toward me. She extended her hand.

I stood and took it for a handshake. Hers was

thin, with long elegant fingers, and creamy soft skin. Like Mama's. I doubted she'd ever had to pick an entire orchard herself before. She wore only one ring, a horseshoe nail bent into a circle—like ones I'd seen farriers make for children when they shod their ponies.

"It's a deal then, Beatrice—" She paused, clearly expecting me to supply my last name.

"Davis."

"We have an agreement, then, Beatrice Davis. You can stay while you help pick the peaches. It'll take a few days. I have thirty-some trees. Go get your things. You can stay in the boys' room upstairs where there are twin beds, so you can be together. Quick, at a canter. We have work to do, don't we?"

CHAPTER 8

It's the stretching up to pluck a peach and then leaning over to put it gently in a basket that wears a body out. They'd gotten so dangerously ripe we had to be extra-special careful, cradling each peach in our palms as we twisted to loosen the stem. Then we gingerly placed them one atop another to not bruise and ruin them.

That and the gnats. Hundreds of them, I swear. Poor Vivian cried a couple of times when those stupid insects lodged themselves in her eye.

Three hours in and I was already a little trembly with fatigue.

When she thought no one was looking, Mrs. Scott put her hand to her back and stretched, rotating her shoulders, grimacing. I did some quick math. Mama would have been thirty-six years old. Mrs. Scott's daughter was likely the same age since they were roommates. That had to make Mrs. Scott around sixty. She seemed pretty nimble, but this work was hard enough for young bodies. She didn't complain, though, even when she didn't see the yellow jacket sucking on a peach and got stung. Just went into the house and came back out, her hand wrapped to hold a poultice of wet baking soda to draw out the venom. She went right back to work.

Getting the peaches from the tippy top of the tree took a ladder. Ralph picked those. Malachi stayed by the truck, emptying our full baskets, one peach at a time, into wooden crates, handling them as tenderly as if they were baby birds.

Even with all of us working steadily, it took over an hour a tree. Around two o'clock we finally broke and sat in the grass, eating biscuits filled with egg salad. And, of course, a few peaches.

"Mm-hmm, these are fine peaches this year, Mrs. Scott. Your daddy would have made an excellent brandy with them."

Vivian gaped. "Your daddy was a bootlegger?" she blurted.

Mrs. Scott startled.

"Ha-ha-ha," Ralph broke into a resounding belly laugh. The man had been burned and bronzed through decades of working in the sun, so his face was carved with wrinkles and freckles that blended into a happy starburst radiating out from his grin. His silver-gray eyes totally disappeared as he guffawed.

He buttoned his mirth, though, when Mrs. Scott replied, her voice sharp, "My father was the county's commonwealth's attorney and a gentleman farmer. He made peach brandy here as his father and his father before him had done. As good as what President Washington had made at Mount Vernon, the local elders said. Liquor wasn't against the law then." She nodded toward the stable hand.

"Ralph used to help mind the fermentation."

"Double-distilled in copper pots I had to keep heated by wood fires," Ralph explained. "Now if you had a mind to make some brandy, Mrs. Scott, and sell it on the downlow to some of those rich, good-timing New Yorkers moving here for the hunt, you'd probably make all you need to pay off your taxes and farm loan. I hear one of them people built a huge stable, shaped like a horseshoe. Now, where those folks getting that kind of money these days?"

"That family? Oil, tobacco, street railways. The other tycoons riding the train down to hunt—tires, baking powder, chemicals, mouthwash, department stores. And now they think they'll make even more fortune breeding racehorses." Mrs. Scott stood and brushed off her pants. I'd seen her frown—big—when Ralph mentioned taxes. "No matter how foolhardy Prohibition is, Ralph, it's the law. I just have to find another way to pay off the bank. Malachi and I will take this truckload of peaches into Middleburg this afternoon. I'm hoping we can get three cents apiece for them—if

I bargain well. Or perhaps I trade them for flour or grain. Tomorrow we'll take what we pick into Leesburg. Then maybe Purcellville."

"What about Washington, Mrs. Scott? Them city people don't have peaches. We could sell them by the Capitol building like me and my sons used to do our vegetable stand. Hungry congressmen and all. Bet they'd give a whole nickel for a peach this pretty."

"That trip would require a great deal of gas," Mrs. Scott answered quietly, but it seemed like she was thinking on it. I was beginning to see it was a hard task to read her. She had such forced composure.

I looked back to Ralph to see if he would press his point. That would be my way of doing things. But he didn't. He just let the suggestion sit there. I made note of the strategy for later.

Straightening her back, Mrs. Scott walked to the next tree, bowed over with peaches. "Let's get one more tree done before we go into town."

Before leaving, Mrs. Scott went upstairs to change. And before she did that, she stood silently studying me. Again. I got twitchy nervous, worrying what she was thinking. I stared back.

Finally, she said, "Come with me. Both of you."

Taking Vivian's hand, I followed Mrs. Scott up the wide staircase, along the landing with its massive window and cushioned window seat, to a sunny room with a fancy oriental rug and wrought iron twin beds. She gave us towels and a bar of soap and told us to wash up in the hall bathroom.

"Don't be luxuriating and using a lot of water. It hasn't rained for nine days, and I am concerned about the well. It dried up altogether during that terrible drought two years ago. So mind what I say."

"Yes, ma'am," we murmured, awed at the sight of a big clawfoot tub. I couldn't even remember the last time we'd taken a bath.

"Beatrice, you seem to understand negotiating. I'd like you to come with me. The owner of the A&P has a soft spot for children." She assessed me again. "Do you have a clean dress?"

My face flushed as red-orange as the peaches. The few clothes I carried in my little suitcase all needed a decent washing.

One more assessing gaze. "I think I still have something that would fit you. Look on the bed when you get out of the tub. Scrub well, please. Fifteen minutes. No more. We need to reach town before five o'clock."

"Yes, ma'am."

"Vivian, I am assuming you can amuse yourself until we return? You can stay in the bedroom or the porch off it. There is a shelf filled with Robert Louis Stevenson."

"Oh yes, ma'am," she chirped.

In the bathroom, I about cried at the feel of warm water and soap suds. I would have lingered for an hour if I could have. I left Vivian in the tub blowing bubbles from her hands and giggling, and scooted to the bedroom, feeling that clock ticking downstairs.

On the bed was a linen dress with a sailor collar and drop-waist and a long, pleated skirt, crisp and lovely when I slipped it on. It smelled of mothballs. Had to have belonged to my mama's roommate when she was my age. I did a tally. Mrs. Scott seemed to have two sons and one daughter, at least. And a husband at some point to have had them. But where were they all now? I wondered especially about the daughter, since according to Daddy she was the one I should appeal to.

I wondered even more when I saw Mrs. Scott's face tighten at the sight of me in the dress. Scowling, she turned and walked briskly to the back door, tossing over her shoulder, "Hurry along now."

In the truck, I sat wedged between Mrs. Scott and Malachi. Stuttering and belching smoke, jolt-bouncing over dirt roads gutted with holes, the jalopy made so much noise, Mrs. Scott had to almost shout as she drove. "Malachi, I need you to stay by the truck as I talk things over with Mr. Craig at the A&P. We'll keep one bushel separate in case people want to buy one or two peaches off the truck. You, young lady, will come inside with me. You keep that serious sad expression no matter what I say, all right?"

"Yes, ma'am." Is that what I looked like?

We passed other old estates, rimmed with hand-stacked stone fences overgrown with honeysuckle. In some fields, corn was just beginning to show, dairy cows grazed in others. Long dusty lanes shaded by walnut trees led to the fieldstone houses. Just like Mrs. Scott's.

Suddenly she slammed on the brakes. My forehead almost hit the dashboard from the lurch. "Of all the impertinent—" Mrs. Scott jumped out of the truck to the ground. "Malachi, hand me the hammer that's in the glove compartment."

She took it from him through the window and marched up a knoll to a wooden sign.

"What's she doing?" I whispered.

"Is there a billboard?" he asked.

"Yes."

"That explains it. Mrs. Scott is running a one-lady 'clean up Middleburg' campaign. Last month, she and Ralph collected a truckload of trash along the road and dumped it on the mayor's doorstep when he said there was no town money for garbage collection."

My mouth popped open. "Why she'd do that?"

"To make a point. She does that. She hates billboards in particular because people are just sticking signs up willy-nilly along the road—'uglifying our lovely vista,' she says. It all started when some fool put up a sign for tobacco by the entrance to her house. He's lucky she didn't see him do it, or he'd likely have some buckshot in his buttocks. She's been on a rampage ever since."

I eyed the offending sign and couldn't help smiling a little at its silly poem.

He played a sax, had no B.O.

But his whiskers scratched, so she let him go.

Buy Burma Shave.

WHAM! Mrs. Scott hit the billboard from behind, popping one corner out from its stakes.

WHAM! The sign fell to the ground with a clatter.

Climbing back into the truck, Mrs. Scott acted as if she'd done nothing unusual. I was trying hard not to gape at her. "We'll pick that up on the way back and use it for firewood," she announced, turning over the ignition.

Pop! The truck rattled on.

A few minutes later, we entered the backend of a small town. A blacksmith's shop, a five and dime, one service station next to it, a bank, a movie theater announcing it was fixing to reopen, a hardware and feed store, a pharmacy, and a gift store called the Iron Jockey.

"I hear there are two Greek brothers come to town to open a deli, Mrs. Scott," said Malachi. "They might like some peaches for cobbler. Folks will be curious and testing them out, 'specially since they're calling it the New York Café. Nothing better than peach cobbler to impress new customers."

"Good idea. We'll try them next trip." She pulled along the front of the A&P.

Before stepping out of the truck, Mrs. Scott checked herself in the truck's rearview mirror, pulling on a tight-fitting, mauve-colored cloche hat with a purple grosgrain rosette on its side. Its bell shape pressed her gray bobbed waves into soft wispy curls around her face, accenting her striking Katherine Hepburn–like high cheekbones. Its color turned the dark blue of her eyes violet. She didn't seem to notice the change, but I sure did. She looked different—pretty even.

Mrs. Scott climbed out and to the ground, straightened her jacketed, tailored dress, and motioned for me to follow. "Did you ever jump that pony of yours?" she asked me quietly.

"Oh, yes, ma'am," I instantly felt that happy surge, that moment of hanging in the air, and smiled.

"Good. This is like riding to a fence. No stopping or not paying attention. You might have to change leads in the middle of the course. No showing you might be scared. Here we go."

CHAPTER 9

As we entered, Mrs. Scott waved at two men behind counters, wearing ties and bleach-clean butcher aprons. She smiled. Smiled! She had dimples! "Hello, Elmer. Huck. Mr. Craig about?"

"In the back, ma'am. I'll get him for you."

"Millicent!" A robust man appeared, wiping his enormous hands before taking hers and kissing her on the cheek. "Now, who's this sweet little thing with you? I swear, in that dress, she reminds me of Marjorie. Oh! I'll be darned. Is she—"

"A visitor," Mrs. Scott supplied abruptly. "This

is Miss Beatrice Davis. I thought she'd enjoy seeing our charming little burg."

"Well now, welcome to town, sweet pea. Help yourself to a penny candy in that jar." He nodded toward the cash register, where sat a glass jar crammed with hard peppermints.

"What can I do for you today, Milly?"

Mrs. Scott patted his hand before pulling hers away from his grasp. "Why, it's what I can do for you, Curtis. I seem to have a bumper crop of peaches this year. Quite lovely. Absolutely perfect, unblemished, and sweeeeeeet," she pulled out the word. "I'm told peaches are fetching a nickel a piece."

"Lord love a duck, who's been telling you fairy tales, Millicent?" Mr. Craig snorted.

Mrs. Scott smiled. "Well, I'm certain I can get that price from your competitor, the Sanitary Grocery. I hear Mr. White has a fine eye for fruit. I just wanted to give you the first chance at them. For old times' sake. They are ripe and ready for pies and canning. I know all the county's best bakers come here. I'd hate for them to feel like they have to go down the street to find good ingredients."

He squinted at her. "One cent a piece."

"Oh, now you're being ridiculous. Well, it was good seeing you, Curtis." She started for the door, wiggling her fingers at me, for me to take her hand. As if we were close and cared for one another.

"Hold on, hold on." Mr. Craig heaved a sigh. "Two cents."

"Three."

"Milly." He stepped close to her again and put his hand on my head, patting it. I didn't care for the familiarity or the way it made me feel like a baby. I was thirteen for goodness' sake. Although I'd gotten so skinny and stuck at the height I was when I was eleven, who'd know. I also knew better than to move and possibly offend him while a bargain was being struck. "I don't have that kind of cash right now. Most everyone is buying on store credit. I extend it to my customers because . . . well, I care about our people. But I might have to lay off one of my boys if people don't start paying their bills. And you know," he lowered his voice even more, "there's a bit of a bill on your account. What about a swap?"

They haggled over flour, sugar, salt, matches, kerosene, coffee.

I kept my face sad and serious through it all, like Mrs. Scott had told me. Then, just as they seemed to be wrapping up, and Mr. Craig was crossing things out in his ledger, Mrs. Scott made eye contact with me, shifting her gaze to some hams wrapped in cheesecloth and then back to me.

I got the cue. I wandered over to that counter and leaned into its glass, my breath fogging it a little, as I looked longingly at the hams. That I wasn't faking at all.

"Oh, child. I know it's been a while since you've enjoyed a little meat. Let's see . . . oh dear . . . maybe I could sacrifice the sugar . . ." Mrs. Scott paused, as if she were flummoxed.

I turned my gaze to Mr. Craig, making my eyes as big as Vivian's when she was hungry or scared.

We left with the ham, too. At special discount, said Mr. Craig, joking—only so much—that Mrs. Scott would pick him clean like a crow would a cornfield if he wasn't careful. But he pinched my cheek, friendly as could be. "You get some meat on those thin bones of yours, sweetie. You look like a string bean."

"Well done," Mrs. Scott murmured as we exited and headed to the truck. She almost smiled for real.

~

As Elmer and Huck hauled away the peaches and loaded in what Mrs. Scott had traded them for, we heard a shouting and honking coming from the western side of town.

People stepped out of storefronts to stand along Washington Street near us.

"What in blue blazes?" muttered a man in a straw boater hat.

"What's coming, Mrs. Scott?" Malachi asked, straining to look down the road. I wondered just how far and what he could see.

Three pickup trucks, driving slow, crammed full of men. A couple dozen more walking alongside the vehicles. Some in full uniforms from the Great War, most wearing beat-up doughboy army caps. All of them gaunt. Hand-painted signs were tied to the truck railings, saying: *The Bonus Expeditionary Forces March on Washington.*

The trucks stopped in front of the ancient tavern in the center of town.

One of the riders climbed onto the hood of the first truck. "Who among you are veterans of Europe's battlefields?"

A handful of men, in their early thirties to forty came forward. Including Malachi. He'd fought in the war?

"Join us! We're marching to the Capitol to ask Congress and President Hoover to pay the bonus America promised us for fighting. The bonus is guaranteed due in 1945, but a lot of us will be dead and gone by then. We need it now. When times are tough. To feed our families. Am I right?"

The men in the truck cheered and the Middleburg residents who were veterans nodded. Including Malachi.

"We answered the call when our country needed us, didn't we?"

Again, the men cheered. Louder. "That we

did!" "Amen!" "Darn tootin'." A few started singing, "*Over there, Send the word, send the word over there, That the Yanks are coming . . .*"

The speaker held up his hands to quiet them. "We're lobbying our congressmen to vote yes to the Bonus Bill that's up in the House this week. Some of us have come all the way from Ohio. March with us! The more of us, the louder our voice."

More cheers.

"They look like scarecrows, poor souls," Mrs. Scott murmured.

A man who'd come out of the bank, stuffing cash into his wallet, came to stand next to us, saying, "Don't be feeling sorry for them, Mrs. Scott."

"And why not, Mr. Carlson?" she asked.

He pulled out his pipe, filled it with some tobacco, and lit it. "I've heard about this. Already a couple thousand of them camping out in abandoned buildings by the Capitol. A bunch of vagrants. Agitators. Probably even communists and socialists."

Mrs. Scott shot him a withering look.

Another man had sauntered up as this Mr. Carlson was talking. "Awww, Fred," the new man said, "these boys served our country. Made the world safe for democracy. Like my son." He paused. "Like Mrs. Scott's boys."

I shot a quick glance at Mrs. Scott to see her reaction for a clue about her family.

But she just pressed her lips tight together as the new man thought a moment, gazing at the veterans. "I wonder, Millicent, if I should offer to let them sleep on my farm tonight? They must be exhausted having come all the way from Ohio along the Pike."

"Oh, I think that's a fine idea, William—"

But the first man spat out, "Don't you let these tramps onto your place, Bill. Next thing you know, they'll be on my fields, too, or lolling around in town, beggaring for change. They've got Negroes with them too. I'm going to tell the sheriff to move these bums along."

"Mr. Carlson," Mrs. Scott's voice was icy, "these are soldiers who kept the Huns from those precious fields of yours—which I don't remember your leaving during the war. Now these veterans are marching to ask for what's owed them—exercising their right to petition their elected representatives. They would surely be on their way to Washington at dawn if they rested a while on William's farm. Look how peaceful and respectful they are. What possible harm could they do you?"

"Oh, I know all about your beliefs in marching on Washington, Mrs. Scott. You and your suffragette hen-friends. Just because you ladies got the vote now doesn't mean you understand how things are. Don't be naive—protests like this are meant to stir things up, they're agitating tactics—like what the Bolshevik commies used to topple Russia. You don't want America to be destroyed by some washed-up soldiers who can't seem to do a decent day's work, do you?"

Mrs. Scott turned to face down the man. She barely reached his shoulder, but he squirmed a little under her glare just like I had. Without taking her eyes off him, she said, "Malachi, let's give these brave and noble veterans that last crate of peaches."

Only then did she turn away.

Like I'd told Vivian—scary.

Mr. Carlson let out a low whistle. "No wonder her husband left her," he muttered to the other man. "Come on, Bill, let's find the sheriff."

Mrs. Scott walked on as if she hadn't heard. But I saw her tip her chin up like Vivian did when she was about to stamp her foot and shout *NO!* at me. Clearly, she had heard that mean man bad-mouth her.

"Bless you, ma'am." The marchers tipped their caps and even teared up a bit as we handed them peaches. We ran out long before we got to the last truck. But without any prompting, the veterans started splitting the peaches in half to share.

One of the Black veterans called out to Malachi. "Brother, I saw you step forward. Who'd you serve with?

"The 92nd. You?"

"The 93rd. The 369th Infantry regiment."

"The Harlem Hellfighters?" Malachi asked, clearly impressed.

"Yessir. Fought with the French. At the Marne."

"They letting you march with them?" Malachi nodded toward the white veterans.

"Yessiree. Don't that beat all? It's not like during the war when they didn't want nothing to do with us. This march—we are all in this together. And if Congress does the right thing, I'm owed $600. A dollar and a quarter for every day I served. With that, I could pay off all my bills, even buy some chickens, maybe a milk cow for my girls, and get the electricity turned back on. The chance to get back on my feet from the walloping this Great Depression done me." He smiled. "Join us!"

Malachi frowned, shook his head, pointing to his eyes. "Lost most of my sight. Not comfortable traveling from home."

The trucks started up their engines with backfires and billows of inky smoke. The drivers called to the veterans to switch—those who'd walked into town crammed together in the flatbed to rest, while those who'd ridden dropped to the ground to walk alongside. As the motley parade rolled out, the veterans began singing:

America! America!
God shed His grace on thee
And crown thy good with brotherhood
From sea to shining sea!

Malachi stood still, listening until he could no longer hear their song. Mrs. Scott waited.

"Mrs. Scott," he said quietly. "If they win this fight, and I get that money, I could—"

"Take it straight to the bank and set up an account for yourself," she cut him off and changed the subject. "Do you want to go into town for this march on the Capitol? I could drive you. Take a load of peaches, as Ralph suggested."

"Thank you, but no, ma'am." His voice became hoarse, "Not after the last time I was in a parade as a soldier." He turned on his heel, ran his hand along the truck until he came to the passenger side.

Mrs. Scott sighed, motioning for me to get in.

Seemed to be an awful lot of sad mysteries hanging about these folks, like a thick fog that is near impossible to navigate without tripping and busting something. How was I supposed to find Viv's and my way in that?

CHAPTER 10

"I know something you don't know," Vivian singsonged as she jumped on my bed and bounced.

I was already half asleep, worn to the bone exhausted. "Leave off, Viv. Can't you see how tired I am." I pulled the pillow over my head.

A pillow. A real feather pillow.

She jerked it away. "Well, I'm tired too." She nestled in beside me, swallowed up in a boy's old nightshirt that Mrs. Scott had told us we'd find in the drawers of the bedroom bureau. "You'll want to hear it. It was a compliment to you."

"From who?" I murmured, still in a half-sleep haze. "Whom," I corrected myself. I could tell that in Mrs. Scott's house, I'd better use proper grammar.

"Mr. Ralph. He thinks you are a natural born horsewoman." Vivian nodded in emphasis.

"What were you doing down at the stable? Didn't Mrs. Scott tell you to stay in the bedroom or the porch? You better mind her. I don't think she likes being contradicted."

"Yes, but . . . you were gone so long, and it was so pretty this afternoon. And . . . and anyway. I got clues, Bea. Like Nancy Drew in *The Hidden Staircase*! Mr. Ralph said that if you were smart about it, that was the way of charming Mrs. Scott—through the horses."

"What else did Mr. Ralph say?"

"Well." Vivian smiled, knowing she had me now. "He said Mrs. Scott is famous around here for breeding and training horses. He says she has such a good seat that she won a massive, persnickety horse on a bet that she couldn't carry an open umbrella while riding him. The horse had thrown a whole bunch of men who hunt fox all the time. They dared her. And she won."

Umbrellas terrify even the most passive of horses. "Are you sure?" I remembered Mrs. Scott implying that Ralph spun some tales.

"Honest. That's what Mr. Ralph said, and he said he'd known Mrs. Scott since, and I quote, 'she was knee-high to a grasshopper.' And she made a lot of money when she sold that fractious horse back to the man who lost the bet—all schooled and agreeable after she worked with him for a while!"

"So why aren't there more horses here now, if she's such an expert horse-trainer?"

Viv shrugged. "Mr. Ralph got kind of funny after that. All he would tell me is that she hates that chestnut and calls him the Black Tuesday Horse."

I frowned. "For the day the stock market crashed?"

Vivian nodded solemnly. "Mr. Ralph says that horse has bad-awful kismet. Like he was cursed.

That everything—for Mrs. Scott and the country—went wrong the day that chestnut stepped his hooves on this place."

I gave my sister a skeptical look. She was spending too much time with that Ouija board.

"No, really, Bea. Mr. Ralph said Mrs. Scott bought the chestnut that very morning, hours before the bottom fell out of Wall Street. Paid way too much money for him, which is unlike her, Mr. Ralph said—made everything worse when the Depression hit full on because she had no savings stocked up. He says that the horse is also why Mrs. Scott isn't riding. And the reason Mrs. Scott and her daughter don't speak anymore."

My heart sank. So appealing to Mrs. Scott's daughter the way Daddy expected wasn't an option. Mrs. Scott and her daughter not speaking sure sounded like when she lost her temper it was final. And that mentioning her daughter and our connection to her through Mama might set Mrs. Scott off. I remembered the flash of anger—or something—on Mrs. Scott's face when she saw me wearing what clearly was once her daughter's dress.

I rubbed my forehead. We better be useful around the farm, then, if we had a snowball's chance in Hades of staying.

"Go to sleep, Viv. We've got a bunch of peaches to pick tomorrow. And we need to do it well." I nudged her a little. "No monkey business, you hear?" But Vivian was already asleep on my shoulder.

We worked seven days straight picking those peaches. Mrs. Scott traded some for grain at the hay and seed store and then harangued a few grocers in Leesburg and Purcellville into giving her two pennies a peach. I didn't count them, but I'd say there was near on a hundred peaches per tree. The orchard had thirty-two trees—meaning we'd plucked and lugged more than three thousand peaches. No wonder my arms ached!

Mrs. Scott said she could pay off several months of back-due electricity bills with the cash those peaches had brought and have a handful of pennies left over. Not enough for all the other bills or taxes, she'd murmured, her brow furrowing into a frown, but at least she didn't have to go through the humiliation of begging to keep her lights on. She seemed pretty pleased about that. So I was hopeful she was pleased with Viv and me, too. Although I knew better than to just hope. That hadn't gotten me anywhere in the past year.

I needed to find other chores Mrs. Scott could use doing.

There was a small vegetable plot—string beans, yellow squash, zucchini, lima beans, tomatoes, cucumbers—that needed weeding and picking. And Lord knows the flowerbeds in her boxwood gardens needed serious work. She'd also kept three bushels of peaches to jar for the winter. That took substantial time in the kitchen. Mrs. Scott didn't seem much interested in cooking, and it would be hard for Malachi to ladle sliced peaches into mason jars without spilling some, what with his eyes. Surely all those things balled up together would keep Viv and me useful to her. Maybe . . .

maybe I could even help Ralph with the horses. The thought of that made me smile, in spite of myself.

Still, the threat of Mrs. Scott calling the sheriff about us haunted me—especially after hearing that blowhard in the village say he was going to set the law on those peaceable war veterans. If the sheriff would do that, how sympathetic would he be to two stray children?

These worries were raging in my head the day after we finished picking those peaches. Mrs. Scott was preoccupied with her *Loudoun Times Herald* at breakfast, so I'd quick-herded Viv out of the house, thinking that out of sight, out of mind with Mrs. Scott would give me time to practice my argument for keeping us around. We were sitting in high grass down by the horse pastures, making clover chains the way Vivian had been asking to do ever since we'd arrived. She'd already made a necklace for me and a crown for herself and was working on bracelets. I swear that child is half fairy.

"Young ladies?"

I startled, totally caught by surprise. That woman moved like a cat on the prowl. "Yes, ma'am?"

Mrs. Scott opened her mouth but paused as I jumped to my feet, my clover necklace swinging. *An almost smile?*

Vivian scrambled to her feet as well. "Hey, Mrs. Scott. We're making clover jewelry." She held up two threads of tiny white blossoms. "Want one?" In her happy puppy-dog way, Vivian skipped forward to tie one on Mrs. Scott's wrist.

I held my breath. What would I do if she refused and hurt Vivian's feelings? I felt my big-sister hackles rise. Which was about the stupidest thing I could do given the circumstances.

Mrs. Scott considered Vivian. Then me.

Vivian smiled.

Mrs. Scott held out her arm to let Vivian tie a knot, green stem to green stem, to hang the clover chain on her wrist. "Thank you, child." She cleared her throat. "Beatrice, I need to speak to you." She glanced at Vivian again, who had already plopped down to pick more clover. "Let's go back to the house."

As we walked, Mrs. Scott said quietly, "Best tell your sister that 'hay' is for horses. Not a greeting. The way someone speaks creates a first impression that will be important to you both when you are older."

"Yes, ma'am."

I expected her to take the childish clover chain off. But she didn't.

She led me to her study. I anticipated something scary, austere—like a courtroom. Instead, it was a surprisingly cozy and disorganized room ringed with floor-to-ceiling bookshelves, crammed all hodgepodge with books and photographs of Mrs. Scott holding silver trophy plates in one hand and beautiful horses, ribbons hanging from their bridles, with the other. There were also pictures of two young men in the same pose—almost identical in their appearance. A girl with a pony. All three of them with Mrs. Scott's distinctive sculpted cheekbones and dimples.

I took all this in as Mrs. Scott sat down behind

a large wooden desk to face me. She gestured to a wingback chair covered in faded chintz. I sat.

"You are to be congratulated on what a hard worker you are, young lady. I am impressed, but—"

I knew what "but" usually meant. "Mrs. Scott," I interrupted as politely as I could, scootching myself to the edge of the chair. "I was noticing that you have a vegetable garden that will need picking. And . . . your boxwood garden is beautiful but . . . ," I hesitated, not knowing if she'd be insulted if I said it was choked with weeds. "It . . . it could use . . . a little bit of love . . . a few weeds pulled?"

She leaned back and folded her arms, her round violet-blue eyes unreadable, not helping me out at all, but she was listening.

"And . . . Mr. Malachi . . . if he's going to be making peach preserves or jarring them for the winter, I bet he could use a little help since he . . . since . . ." I trailed off. I still didn't understand what their relationship was or what troubled his eyes.

Mrs. Scott shifted a bit, an arched gray eyebrow rising. "Go on."

"I used to help my mama in the kitchen, and she showed me how to can things for the winter."

Pressing her lips together for a moment—which I had come to recognize was a sign she was thinking on something, Mrs. Scott asked, "Your mama was a good cook?"

"Oh, yes, ma'am," I said with reverence.

She nodded slightly to herself. "I have been annoyed by those weeds," she muttered. "My father would be appalled." She gazed out the window, continuing her conversation with herself in a whisper I had to strain to catch. "Can't afford a gardener. Can barely keep Ralph and Malachi employed. Curse that chestnut. If I hadn't—" She shook her head and went silent.

I made myself wait it out, although I felt like I'd stepped onto an anthill and angry insects were swarming all around us.

Finally, Mrs. Scott turned to face me, cocking her head, and spoke more obviously to me. "Perhaps we could extend our arrangement for a bit."

She raised her pointer finger, as I caught my breath in relief. "For a bit, I say. But did your father divulge where he was going to look for work? That way I or the sheriff could alert him that you are well and safe. I don't feel right your being here without his knowing."

I hadn't anticipated that kind of question—just a threat of sending us packing to some state-run children's home for orphans. No quick fib came to me. Did Daddy even care if we were well and safe? Did he?

She was saying something, but I couldn't hear Mrs. Scott's words at all, just an anxious ringing in my ears, when suddenly Vivian was in the room, her face red, her dress torn, sobbing, coughing out her words.

"I'm sorry, I'm sorry, I'm so sorry." She looked at Mrs. Scott with terror, but she held her ground. "I wanted to put a clover chain on the horses' necks . . . the mare loved hers . . . but the chestnut . . . oh, he is a mean beast, Mrs. Scott . . . he backed me into the corner of his stall and . . . and bit at me and ripped my sleeve and reared and . . . and Mr. Ralph rushed in . . . and . . ."

Mrs. Scott was already on her feet.

"Mr. Ralph got kicked. He's . . . he's having a hard time breathing . . ."

Mrs. Scott bolted out the door as Vivian grabbed my hand and tugged. "He needs help, Bea. I . . . I might have killed him."

CHAPTER 11

Sprinting, we reached the stable doors, to find the chestnut standing over Ralph, collapsed on the aisle floor. That murderous horse was nuzzling the hurt stable hand, the way nice horses do when a pasture mate has gone down in the field.

"Stop." Mrs. Scott held out her arms to bring Viv and me to a sudden halt. "If we startle that hellion, he could rear and come down on Ralph again." She moved slowly and kept her voice sweet, even though she was using a bucketload of bad names. "Easy, you ——, easy now, ———."

She glanced from the horse to Ralph, back to the horse. "Ralph, can you hear me?"

No answer.

She was halfway down the aisle when the chestnut snorted, shook his head, and reared up anyway, out of spite.

I've never seen anyone move that fast, waving her arms and shouting all manner of curses as she threw herself down to cover Ralph, frightening the horse so that he wheeled on his rear legs and bolted down the aisle and out the other end of the stable. Had he come straight down, he would have cut up Mrs. Scott—bad.

"Ralph?" Mrs. Scott sat back and quickly assessed his wounds. A long gash and a growing purplish bruise on his forehead. His left arm lying awkwardly. His breathing raspy and fitful, his right hand clutching his side.

"Beatrice, get some saddle pads out of the tack room and a wicking blanket. Be quick about it! Vivian, run to Malachi. Tell him to call Dr. Liburn, that it's an emergency. Tell him Ralph was kicked. He's probably cracked some ribs and is having trouble breathing. His arm looks broken, and he may have a concussion. I need the doctor to come as soon as possible. Do you understand? As soon as humanly possible."

Vivian nodded, tears streaming down her face.

"Hurry!" Mrs. Scott barked.

Vivian turned and ran.

To me she said, "Put those pads under his head and his shoulders as I lift him. Gently now." She lowered her voice to speak to Ralph as she cradled his head. "I am going to shift you, just a little."

No answer. Ralph just groaned as we propped him up with the fleece. But he started to breathe a bit easier.

We did the same with his arm. Covered him with the light cotton sheet, meant to help a horse dry off after a bath. Still no word from him.

"Ralph." Mrs. Scott took his unhurt right hand and whispered, "Don't you be leaving me, too. You hear me? Please."

His eyelids fluttered, opened, shut.

"Ralph, please," Mrs. Scott's voice snagged.

"Don't you be worrying, Miss Milly," he

murmured. "You just need to get back up on that horse now. Don't let your daddy see you afraid."

Mrs. Scott bit her lip. Tears filled her eyes. "Ralph?"

His breathing was peaceful now. But he had passed out.

She didn't let go of his hand and she wouldn't look up at me. I could see Mrs. Scott shudder, muttering over and over, "Curse that horse."

All I could think about was that could have been Vivian on the ground, sliced and broken.

We stayed frozen like that, me in a storm of big-sister guilt, until Vivian reappeared, pulling Malachi along by the hand. "Mrs. Scott?" he called out. "The doctor said he'd be here in twenty minutes."

"Thank God," she murmured. Only then did Mrs. Scott look up at me. "How good of a rider are you?"

Startled by the question, I fumbled, "I . . . I . . ."

"Can you handle a canter in the open on a quiet horse?"

"Yes, ma'am."

"Go get the saddle and bridle with the nameplate *Sweet Charity* and tack up the mare. Take a halter and lead line with you and see if you can find that hellion horse—before he hurts someone else. He seems to respond to you, and every horse quiets down around Charity. If he cooperates, and it seems safe, get that line on him and lead him back, riding her. Do you think you can do that?"

"Yes, ma'am."

She nodded. "Go on, then."

As I stood, I'm pretty sure I heard her mumble, "And then I'll do what I should have done before—send that vicious creature to the glue factory."

How long had it been since the mare had been ridden? Even the most generous horse can get ornery after months of neglect. No time to ease into it, though.

Saddle pad, saddle on top of it. The mare stamped a little.

Girth, under her belly and buckled to the saddle's billets. Cinched up like a belt to hold the saddle in place—not too sudden, not too tight to make her think I was unkind or thoughtless. The mare turned and pushed me with her head—a protest but not a serious one.

I put the bridle's cold bit into her velvety mouth. Most horses fight that. Some refuse to unclench their teeth unless you stick your thumb into a secret pocket behind their molars. But she accepted the metal mouthpiece with hardly any resistance other than a snort and shake of her head.

Sweet Charity. Her name sure fit.

In five minutes flat, I had my foot in the stirrup and swung up on her back, walking us in the direction that crazed chestnut had bolted.

Trotted. Bouncy.

And then, oh glorious, a canter.

I had no business feeling any kind of happiness given Ralph lying hurt and unconscious because of my little sister and her fairy-child nonsense. But I couldn't help a little gasp of joy as that sweet old mare kicked up into an easy, rolling canter, as if she knew we were on a mission and needed to hurry. *Hurry.*

Charity even tolerated my finding my seat again, after two years of not riding at all, to make my body relax and hips rock with her three-beat stride so I stopped popping up and down in the saddle—hurting her back.

I know I shouldn't admit it—it was so insensitive in the circumstances—but I felt life flood back into me, sailing through the air on that horse. And I rejoiced.

Giving Charity a loose rein, figuring she had a much better idea where that chestnut might run, I threaded my fingers into a fistful of her mane to make sure I stayed on if she made a sudden turn.

She cantered up a long hill, down its other side, through high grasses and feathery Queen Anne's lace just starting to bud, into a grove of sycamores. There she slowed to a careful trot, then a walk, as she picked her way down a pebbly path to a creek, sparkling and gurgling in shallows. She stopped, ankle-deep in the cool water, and drank, slurping contentedly, like this was a favorite place of hers that she had sorely missed. She pawed a bit, and I tapped my heels on her side to get her to move on. Some horses love to roll in water. Pawing like that is a sure sign they're considering doing it even though a rider is on their back. I could almost hear her thinking, *oh, all right, killjoy.*

Her ears pricked up.

"What is it, girl?" Then I heard it too. Something very large, splashing. Down the creek, I could spot sprays of water, a flash of red. There he was.

"Come on." I clucked and we walked forward along the creek bed, Charity threading herself among the rocks. She whickered lightly in greeting.

Hearing her, the chestnut rose from the water, dripping, glistening, lit by a shaft of light coming through the trees. Mystical, majestic—like a unicorn in some fairy tale.

Charity tossed her head. He neighed back, loud and long, all boy-horse bluster, and began trotting toward us.

For a moment, I couldn't believe my luck—that he seemed so enchanted by Charity that he was going to come right to me, easy-peasy.

Then I realized how much danger I was in. I was surrounded by rocks, a few boulder-size. If he charged, or she spun in fear of him, I could fall off and crack my head open on any of them.

And that's when the chestnut picked up speed.

CHAPTER 12

He lunged through the water, vaulting over rocks, landing and skidding on pebbles lining the creek bed. Was that horse insane? Any one of those moves could snap his front legs.

He didn't stop.

Alarmed, Charity shook her head and did a little half rear, telling me to get us the heck out of there. I opened the rein to turn her, but she did exactly what I had feared—she whipped to the side suddenly, throwing me akimbo.

I swayed to the left, then to the right. Lost the

reins, lost the stirrups. I felt myself sliding off. It would be an awful way to go—whacked against rocks and trampled in shallows. Blindly, I grabbed her mane with both hands and wrapped my legs as tightly as I could on her flanks as she plunged, splashing, through the water to the embankment.

That deranged chestnut kept coming.

He sailed over a boulder to come up on Charity's rear. She cow-kicked a warning at him. I lurched up out of the saddle, my head hitting her neck as her rump lifted and her back legs lashed out. The only reason I didn't flip and go flying over her head was she came down fast from that back-kick, like a seesaw switching, to surge straight up the high bank.

Thrashing through ferns, trampling bluebells, she crashed through low-growing pawpaw trees. I buried my face in my arms to avoid my eyes being skewered by the branches she was snapping off in her panicked dash.

The chestnut followed right behind her, neighing.

Charging out of the tree line to open fields,

Charity was winded now, her neck lathered with sweat, and heaving to breathe. How old was she exactly? How long could she hold up without collapsing?

The chestnut was only a few strides away.

Without my feet in them those iron stirrups were pounding poor Charity's side, like I was kicking her cruelly, driving her into a frantic gallop. They were beating my legs all up, too, clipping my ankles so hard I cried out in pain. I had to get my feet back into those stirrups or I was going to fall, and she might run so hard her heart could burst. It happens with racehorses more than people want to tell.

For God's sake, young lady, find those stirrups.

I'm not sure how I did it, to be honest—except Charity wasn't *trying* to throw me, even in her frenzy—but I managed to trap the stirrup leathers under my thighs and find those iron bells with my toes. Left stirrup, foot in. Right stirrup, in. I could feel Charity calm a little.

But the chestnut was right on her tail, pressing her on.

Gasping, I realized we were heading for one of those piled stone walls. Four feet high maybe. Charity would never clear it. At this breakneck speed, I was too terrified to let go of her mane to try grabbing for the reins.

We were within thirty strides of that fence.

Whoa, Charity, whoa.

Twenty.

I was going to die.

Who would take care of Vivian?

Mama, please.

Then something happened that if I hadn't witnessed it, been saved by it, I would say was wishful hooey.

Up from the other side of the wall popped a young fox. A teenage cub, lean and spry, innocent and vulnerable. Then another. And another. They were venturing out from their den to play together in the sunshine—unsuspecting of the danger barreling toward them.

We were going to crash right into them as well as all that unyielding stone.

Whoa, Charity, whoa. Please whoa.

Ten strides.

Suddenly, in a brilliant flash of red, the mama fox vaulted up into the air, landing on the fence in front of them, barking a warning at us.

Startled, Charity spooked and—*thank God*—veered.

The chestnut thundered by us as the cubs and their mama scattered. He sailed over that wall, with a foot of air under him to spare.

Charity came to a stop, heaving.

I grabbed back the reins and stroked her neck. "Good girl, that's it, steady," I murmured, shaking from my fright as much as she was panting.

I was alive.

I only reveled in that wonderment for a moment, though. I had failed. The chestnut was nowhere to be seen. What would I tell Mrs. Scott?

Hello orphanage.

Well, at least I could keep from making Charity sick. I needed to get her heart rate back down to normal, which meant she needed a sponge bath to cool her off. We had to go back to the barn. I could see it in the distance. I slid to the ground to take my weight off her and loosened her girth so she could breathe easier. Then she and I began the long walk back.

What *was* I going to say to Mrs. Scott? Sorry, I almost got your sweet old mare killed. Sorry, I don't know where that hothead chestnut, the one that you paid too much money for, is. Sorry, my sister was childish and careless and got Ralph so beaten up and hurt. Sorry, you now have a doctor's bill to pay. Sorry, my daddy didn't know what to do with us and left us to cause you all sorts of trouble.

I trudged along the stone fence, a sorry-ass flopperoo, looking for a gate.

Sorry. So sorry.

I heard him before I saw him. Hooves drumming, *da-da-dum, da-da-dum, da-da-dum.* The loud rhythmic breathing with each surging stride of a horse pushing himself forward, faster, faster.

Was he coming after us again?

Alarmed, I turned just as the chestnut came

soaring over that stone wall.

Thud. He landed, circled, circled, and jumped it again.

Scrambling, I retightened Charity's girth and swung up into the saddle in case she and I had to make another run for it.

The chestnut thundered along on the other side of the stone wall, only his head visible. Then came another moment of silence as he launched himself a third time, skimming easily over the poison ivy thicket growing along the wall's top that added another half foot of height.

Hitting the ground, he shook his head triumphantly, cavorted in celebration of himself, turned, cantered a few strides, and sailed back over.

My mouth popped open. The chestnut was jumping that huge fence just for fun.

Snorting, Charity pranced in place. As if she wanted to give it a go herself. "Not a chance, old girl." I patted her and waited, bracing myself for trouble. What would that raucous horse do next?

Da-da-dum, da-da-dum, da-da-dum.

Again, the chestnut glided over the stones,

landed, and stopped, swishing and flitting his tail, eyeing Charity with a look-what-I-can-do bravado.

The little nicker she gave him in response felt like laughter. Was it possible that this whole melee was just his trying to play with her?

Seriously? I could have gotten killed for that?

Charity might seem amused, but I was furious, wary, unsure what to do. That chestnut was dangerously unpredictable. And in the mayhem he caused down at the creek and the chase in the field, I'd lost the halter and lead line I was supposed to use on him.

He stood, waiting.

Charity stamped, impatient.

I really did need to get her back for that rubdown. Maybe, now that the chestnut seemed to have run himself out, he would simply follow her back to the stable. There was nothing to do but try. The clock was ticking in terms of preventing her suffering a sweat chill that could leave her wheezing for days.

I clucked to move Charity forward in a contained walk, steering wide around the chestnut.

"Good girl, easy does it," I crooned. "Eeeeea-sy, now. We're alllll riiight."

The chestnut shadowed, dancing around her, like a colt orbits its mama—all the way back to the barn. As we reached the paddocks, that hell-raiser horse decided to jump those fences, too. In. Out. Back in—where he realized the clover looked good and he lowered his head to graze. As if none of that near-fatal rumpus had happened.

He was a baddy, that one.

CHAPTER 13

I left the chestnut in the pasture to take care of Charity, hoping he'd stay inside the fence until I got back with a halter. Dismounting, I led her to the stable opening, feeling no sense of relief at arriving there in one piece since I was terrified of what I might find inside.

Ralph still lay on the floor but was conscious at least. The doctor's back was turned to me as he wrapped a splint on Ralph's arm. Vivian was cuddled up against Malachi, who sat on a turned-over bucket. Mrs. Scott was pacing, arms crossed.

As soon as she spotted me, she scowled. "Towels are in the tack room. Sponge Charity down and dry her. Immediately."

"Yes, ma'am."

"Where's that fool chestnut?"

"In the paddock. Is . . . is Mr. Ralph going to be okay?"

"Yes," she spoke sharply, "no thanks to—" She broke off. "Just take care of Charity. Mind you do it right."

"Yes, ma'am." I took off Charity's saddle and bridle and hurried toward the tack room, trying not to cry—in embarrassment, in delayed reaction to the danger I'd just survived and the fact that no one asked if I was all right, in fear that Vivian and I were done for with Mrs. Scott.

No. No tears. I could tell Vivian had been crying enough for both of us.

I slowed to pass Ralph quietly, so I wouldn't disturb him, but he reached out with his unhurt hand to touch my ankle. "Young'un," he murmured. "Be sure to give that old beauty a carrot for me, ya hear? Reward her for her hard work. A lump of sugar can work wonders sometimes with the other one, too."

He winked and then closed his eyes with a wince as the doctor tightened the splint.

❧

As I rubbed down Charity, Mrs. Scott and the doctor conferred. He had the oddest accent, a little like British characters in movies I'd seen, but a little French sounding, too. Clipped and songlike at the same time. I'd never heard a voice like that before.

"He cracked a few ribs," the doctor was saying, "and that arm is broken. A simple fracture from what I can feel. I apologize I cannot send him to the hospital for an X-ray to know for sure. As a Black man, I am not permitted to admit my patients there."

"Racist fools," Mrs. Scott muttered.

"I'm not going to no hospital, Doc," Ralph called from the floor. At least there was nothing wrong with his hearing. "Just need some rest to let myself heal. One of my hundreds of hungry grandkids can come mind me for a day or two."

The doctor chuckled.

Mrs. Scott lowered her voice to a whisper. "Doctor, are you sure he would recover—fully—if that's all we did?"

"Ma'am," Ralph was bellowing now. "I done recovered from worse than this before. I'll be right as rain in a week. This ain't nothing."

"Ralph, please let me have this conversation without further interruption," she called back to him.

The doctor laughed again. "He'll heal through sheer stubbornness if nothing else. I'll give you a prescription for a week of painkillers to get him through the initial discomfort. But it's going to be two to three weeks for those ribs. And six weeks minimum for that arm before he should lift anything substantial."

I felt her shoot me a proverbial look that could kill—a shaft of blame that skewered me from behind. After a moment of tense silence, she asked, "But he'll heal?"

"If he takes the time. Yes."

"All right. I'll bring the truck down to the stable to drive him home."

"Now, Mrs. Scott, don't be driving me nowhere," Ralph protested. "It's just a stone's throw. I can walk home like I have every day for near on sixty years now."

God almighty, how old was this man?

"Ralph," the doctor corrected him this time, "you should not walk anywhere except to the kitchen table and the latrine for the next week."

"Awww now, Doc—"

"Ralph, for pity's sake," Mrs. Scott stopped him. "It is decided. I'll get the truck. I am going to pack the seat with a few pillows."

"Now, Mrs. Scott—"

"Hush!" Then she lowered her voice again to address the doctor. "I had to sell the Studebaker. And the truck isn't exactly long on cushioning. Just give me a few minutes, please." She threw a parting shot at Ralph, "Mind the doctor until I get back."

After Mrs. Scott left, I dared to turn around from Charity and insert myself into the conversation to try to make amends for my little sister. "Is there anything I can do to help, Doctor . . . Doctor . . ." I realized I didn't know his name.

He bowed his head slightly. "Dr. Liburn. And your name?"

"Bea . . . Beatrice Davis."

"Nothing at this moment, Beatrice. Although I am sure Mrs. Scott will appreciate your help in the stable as Ralph heals." He strode over to Malachi and Vivian, who looked up at him with such sorrow and regret I ached for her. Dr. Liburn crouched to her height and softly asked, "And who may you be?"

"Vivian," she murmured. Then, leave it to my little sister to ask the rude question: "You talk funny, where are you from?"

The doctor smiled. "From a beautiful little island in the Caribbean—Saint Kitts. Left it long ago, though, on a whaling ship when I wasn't much older than you. Made it to New York City, went to high school in the Bronx. Then served in the war, like Malachi did. Came back to Washington, DC, to study medicine at Howard University. Like Malachi had wanted to, before his eyes were damaged." He paused. "Do you like science, Vivian?"

"I think so?"

"Well, you should. Science is a miracle happening right here on earth. We have cells in our body that know how to heal—as if they came with an instruction book telling them what to do. So . . . don't you worry about Ralph. He will be fine. If," the doctor looked pointedly at Ralph, "if he minds what I say. And if . . . if he knows what's good for him."

"Awww, Doc, what about—"

"And if he remembers what's good for Mrs. Scott—getting himself fully healed so when he comes back, he is strong to work the stable and her horses."

Ralph gave a dramatic sigh and muttered, "I hear you, Doc."

"Good. How are the eyes, Malachi? Still only shadows and shapes?"

"Yes."

The doctor put his hand on Malachi's shoulder. "At least there is that. When retinas detach after a blow to the head it's permanent unless treated immediately. I wish you had found me sooner."

Malachi nodded, grim.

The doctor didn't withdraw his hand. "Malachi," his voice remained gentle—that tone doctors use to share bad news. "I think it best I share something with you before you hear it on the radio."

"Yes?"

"The Bonus Army—"

"Did Congress pass the bonus bill?" Malachi sat up straighter.

"The House did. But the Senate defeated it."

Malachi frowned, bit his lip. "But why?"

Dr. Liburn's expression tightened. "I have my opinions. But . . . there are children present." He paused for several beats, then he squeezed Malachi's shoulder and lowered his voice. "There's more, I'm afraid. President Hoover sent the army to disperse veterans keeping vigil outside the Capitol."

"What?" Malachi gasped. "He turned soldiers on . . . on veterans?"

"Yes." Dr. Liburn's voice stayed contained, but his own angry disbelief bubbled up and came through, even though we children were still very present. "Tanks, tear gas, cavalry with sabers drawn, infantry with fixed bayonets. Chased our veterans down Pennsylvania Avenue. Then the army went to the encampment the veterans had built down in Anacostia. Burned everyone's shelters to the ground."

Malachi knocked the doctor's hand away and shot to his feet, his hands balled into fists. "How could . . . why?"

"I know. It's hard to fathom that kind of coldheartedness." He paused. "Have you heard Franklin Delano Roosevelt speak on the radio? He's running for president against Hoover."

Malachi shook his head.

"Well, I want to find out more about the man. There's a rally for him next Saturday in Leesburg. He's promising a new deal for the American people. Says the federal government to not offer help, a new chance, would be betraying Americans' patience with these terrible times. That we must not be timid. He's pledging his aid not only to what he called the forgotten man, but to the forgotten woman. I like the sound of that. Don't you?"

Malachi nodded.

A new chance. I liked the sound of that too. But I couldn't help wondering if those highfalutin' words would be applied to forgotten children as well? Or if Mrs. Scott was of a mind to think that way—especially about children who caused a berserk horse to near kill a nice old man.

Berserk horse.

I needed to get that unruly chestnut into his stall. Better do it while the doctor was still there in case the horse tried to split my head open too.

By the time I reached the paddock gate—a new halter and lead line in my hand, a carrot in my pocket—I was mad rather than afraid. What the heck was this horse's problem anyway? He was being fed, had a clean, safe stall to sleep in every night. There were about a million Americans who'd sell their souls to be him right now.

I watched the chestnut graze, wondering how best to approach to keep from riling him. He ignored me.

When I slipped in through the gate, though, his head snapped up. He shook it, neighed threateningly, and eyed me with some alarm. I stopped, slowly raising my hands. "Remember me? I'm the one who saved your life."

The chestnut snorted, holding his head high so he could really glare down at me—assessing and warning me off at the same time.

We stayed in that standoff until, with a dismissive stamp of his front hoof, the chestnut went back to grazing. But he kept his eye on me all the same.

Inching forward, I warbled, "Eeeea-sy," over and over. I made it close enough to get the line around his neck, when that blankety-blank horse shied and lunged to the side, just out of reach. But he didn't bolt. He went back to eating clover.

We repeated that annoying dance about ten times.

Finally, I realized he was spinning away from

me only when I raised the halter and line to try to put on him. I dropped them to the grass. Pulled the carrot from my pocket and held it out.

Again, the chestnut's head shot up. He reared, but just a little. Up and right back down, shaking his head.

"You don't scare me."

He snorted.

"You don't. I've seen more trouble than you." I snapped the carrot in two to draw his attention to it.

His snorting turned to curious nickering.

Snap. Snap. I broke the carrot into fourths. He stretched his nose toward me and then pulled back.

I smiled in spite of myself. "Remember our midnight stroll?"

Again, he stretched out his head, nostrils quivering, just far enough that his upper lip could push the carrot pieces around in my outstretched hand, the bristle-like hairs on his chin tickling my palm. But he pulled back without taking a carrot.

Why was he so distrusting?

Why are *you* so distrusting, accused a voice

inside my head as the chestnut stared me down. My turn to snort. At myself. I could act a lot like this riled-up chestnut when I was unsure of a situation. Or a person. "I guess we have things in common," I whispered. "It's okay. It's just a carrot. Eeeea-sy."

The chestnut took a step closer. I did too, holding the carrot bits closer to his muzzle. "Come on. It's all right."

He mouthed one. Pulled back. Fiddled with it again, pushing it around in my hand until—finally—he took the first piece.

Cruuunch-crunch-crunch.

I stroked his neck, moving closer to his side so I could get a hand in his mane. I scratched down along it to his withers, like pasture mates nibble on one another, getting those itches on a friend's neck that a horse can't reach himself.

The chestnut let out a long sigh, his body relaxing. He nuzzled me for the rest of the carrot. I held up my hand, flat, so he didn't mistake one of my fingers for a carrot. As he munched, I reached for the halter. This time he let me slip it on him.

"Good boy," I murmured, and patted his back. That's when I noticed twenty or more dimples running along his rib cage to his belly. Little notches, like a person's cleft chin, all over his side, right beside where a girth would go. What the heck?

Keeping my hands on his neck, I ducked under his head and looked at his other flank. The same. Gently, I ran my hand along his side. He flinched. Suddenly, I knew what those marks were. Scars. From spurs. Someone had jabbed the chestnut brutally to make him go.

A horse like this? That would jump four-foot fences for fun? A horse like this didn't need to be spurred that viciously.

"No wonder." I wrapped my arms around the chestnut's neck. "I won't hurt you, boy," I whispered. "I promise. Come on. Let's go in."

He followed me. All the way into his stall. And a terrible thought came to me: Mrs. Scott was so angry at this horse. Could she have done this to him?

CHAPTER 14

Mrs. Scott was gone for hours.

"Getting Ralph settled in most like," Malachi said. But he furrowed his brow, obviously worried her delay meant Ralph was hurting more than he let on.

Viv too. She was never this quiet.

The longer Mrs. Scott didn't return, the more anxious I got. Ralph's injury was Viv's and my fault. I'd sure want to be rid of such troublemakers—no matter how many peaches we'd picked or weeds we could pull. "Viv, let's surprise Mrs. Scott by cleaning the kitchen. Let's make it sparkle."

I swept. I scoured pots. Glasses. Dishes. Silverware.

Vivian mopped the floor. Wiped down the windows, the cabinets, the inside of the stove. For once she didn't stop in the middle of her tasks.

Malachi carefully put things away after we cleaned them.

No one talked.

Until Malachi dropped a china bowl and it shattered on the floor.

Swearing, he slapped his hand against the wall. Hard enough to rattle the dishes in the cabinet. He stood there, head down, his fists clenched, his face squeezed into a terrible grimace. Pure fury. Trying hard to stuff it down.

I froze. What could I say to a grown man so frustrated? I'd obviously failed with everything I'd said to Daddy to try to cheer him up at such moments. Watching Malachi brought back a flood of horrible images of my father wrestling with guilt, bitterness, shame. I closed my eyes against the memories.

"That's okay, Mr. Malachi. I used to break things all the time when I was little."

My eyes popped open to see Vivian taking Malachi's hand and his startling at her touch.

"It must be hard to do things when you can't see," she said in that earnest voice of hers. "It would make me mad, too. Especially if I lost my vision in a war."

Straightening up Malachi muttered, "Didn't lose my sight in battle. Happened here. During a parade of our regiment, celebrating our bravery in France. White folk didn't think we had the right to honor ourselves like that."

I gasped, putting together the pieces of things I'd heard before. Malachi had been attacked by fellow Americans—white Americans.

"Well, that's silly," Vivian said innocently, not understanding. "My mama always said that a job well done deserved a gold star."

The sigh Malachi let out was long and rattling and made my throat tighten up. "I'll sweep it up," I squeaked. "Mrs. Scott won't . . ." I started to say "mind," but what did I know about what she'd mind or not, or what she'd do when she was hopping mad. "Mr. Malachi, that chestnut horse. I got a good look at—" I broke off again, realizing that saying I "got a good look" at anything was awful insensitive.

"Go on," he said.

"I saw . . . I noticed . . . I mean . . . there are a bunch of little scars all over his sides."

Malachi nodded.

"Did . . . I've seen that . . . I mean, I've noticed Mrs. Scott can be . . . has a bit of a . . . temper. Did . . . did Mrs. Scott do that?" I finally got the question out in a rush.

"What? No. The exact opposite," Malachi answered emphatically. "During a foxhunt, she saw his rider spurring that horse until he bled. The man was determined to lead the pack, and the chestnut was set off by the hounds' ballyhoo. Rearing and refusing. He was young and skittish."

"Still is," I murmured.

"I'm told Mrs. Scott rode up to the man, grabbed his reins, and demanded he get off that horse if he was going to misuse it so brutally.

Caused quite an uproar among the other hunters because she was holding up the chase. Finally, she told the man she'd buy the horse from him if he'd dismount then and there. Offered him a ridiculous amount of money. So much that the man laughed at her. Said she couldn't possibly mean it, that she clearly didn't have any understanding of what it took to make a stubborn horse go."

"That's the thing about Mrs. Scott—if people dare her, or demean her, or she sees them being cruel, she's going to stand up to them. To her own detriment.

"She stuck to her guns. He got off and stormed home. She emptied out her bank account—lean as it already was—to buy that horse. Said she reckoned she could train him to jump beautifully. Compete him at shows that awarded big prize money and make back her investment. Even speculated that he could make it to the National Horse Show. If anyone could achieve that, it's Mrs. Scott. But that very afternoon the stock market crashed. And then . . . she and her daughter—" Malachi broke off. "Well . . . it's not my place to say."

He thought a moment. "Here's the thing. Mrs. Scott employs me despite my blind eyes. She continues to employ Ralph even though none of her horses are being worked. Despite how broke and in trouble financially she is now. I pretty much grew up with Mrs. Scott's boys when my mama was alive and keeping house for her. So I know her well. . . . Just because someone has a temper doesn't mean she is unkind. Mrs. Scott . . . she has a good heart . . . despite all that has happened to her. Despite what went on with Marjorie and that horse."

A good heart. Just like Mama had said, according to Daddy.

Could Viv and I really count on that, I wondered, given Ralph's injuries? Then my own heart did a little jolt. *That horse.* What time was it?

Looking out the window, I saw shadows were already long across the lawn. Twilight was coming. Those horses needed to be fed and turned out. I dashed for the stable.

Following Ralph's routine, I sang and hummed as I dumped the grain—to make the horses feel like nothing was amiss, that there hadn't been a terrible earthquake in their life.

Tiptoe through the window . . .

Scoop.

By the window, that is where I'll be . . .

Scoop. Dump.

Come tiptoe through the tulips with me . . .

"He'll be back," I murmured to Charity as she munched. "Don't worry. He didn't leave you."

When they finished their dinner, I took them out in pairs, just like Ralph did, saving the chestnut for last so I could handle him solo.

Bang!

He was kicking his stall walls as I came back from the field after releasing the two dappled-grays. They'd trotted off together, calm, sweet. Horses could be like that, I reminded myself. They didn't have to be temperamental handfuls. I braced myself for the chestnut's ire.

Bang!

"There's no need for that."

Bang!

"Quit that stuff and nonsense. Eeeeea-sy."

As I pulled back the stall door, the chestnut was mid-rear. But on seeing me, he dropped to the ground, snorted, stepped forward, nudged me, stepped back. Eyed me suspiciously but waited to see what I'd do.

"That's it, boy." I felt myself grin. "We're okay now. You and me." I held up his halter so he could see it before I tried to put it on.

He stamped but lowered his head for me to slip the halter over his ears. Then, prancing, he let me lead him out without dragging me.

As I opened the gate, he bolted through it. Dashed around the pasture, rousting the other geldings into canters while Charity focused on clover. She'd obviously had enough of his shenanigans. Then, after he'd herded and chased everyone else to his braggadocio satisfaction, he turned and galloped back toward me. Gaining speed.

Oh no. No, no, no.

He sailed over the fence, landed within feet of

me, nickered, and bolted down the lane, just as Mrs. Scott's pickup turned into it and started jolting and backfiring toward the house.

No, no, no, no.

I ran after the chestnut. But before I got far, he was thundering back. He slowed from breakneck to a canter, down to a trot, then a walk. And came right to me. Nudged me, hard but friendly, so I staggered only a little. Then he jumped the fence back into the pasture and started grazing beside Charity.

What a troublemaker. But . . . what a jumper. No wonder Mrs. Scott had thought she might be able to train the chestnut to clear any fence, win any competition.

I caught my breath. *Show competition. Prize money.* Could this mercurial, quarrelsome, but beautiful chestnut save Mrs. Scott? And therefore, Viv and me?

The truck door slammed. I ran to catch Mrs. Scott before she went into the house and could call the glue man like she'd threatened. Or the sheriff.

“Mrs. Scott!” I called, waving my arms.

She stopped. Waited. She looked exhausted. “Yes?” her tone was icy.

Winded, I spluttered, “Did you see? Did you see him jump the fence?”

“Yes.”

“He did that earlier today, too,” I raced on, trying to ignore the unspoken “what of it?” in her expression. “Jumped all the stone walls coming back and then in and out of the pasture.”

“Yes. He obviously cannot be controlled. It is time to be rid of him.” She rubbed her forehead, like there were things crawling around up there she wanted to squelch. “And as for you and your sister, I can’t have a child around my stable who doesn’t have the sense to stay away from a—”

I broke in before she could say what was logical and prudent, but spelled doom for Vivian and me. Used what Malachi had told us. “That chestnut is a beautiful jumper, Mrs. Scott. I bet he could win all sorts of shows. With prize money.”

She pursed her lips.

“He just needs a good rider. A rider he likes.

Did you see how he just came back to me? I . . . I think . . ."

"That he likes you?" Mrs. Scott let out a derisive scoff.

I frowned but held my ground.

"Aren't you afraid of him?"

I lied. "No, ma'am."

"That so? Then you haven't the sense God gave a flea."

The kitchen door swung open. Malachi stood in it, Vivian hiding behind him. Not being able to see us in a standoff with all sorts of sparks flying, he called out, "Mrs. Scott! How is Ralph?"

"Not good. His injuries are serious and . . ." She turned away from me to Malachi, whose worried expression seemed to gut punch Mrs. Scott. She stopped mid-sentence. Her tone shifted. "Mostly, he's mad as a wet hen. But settled in at least."

"You were gone so long."

"I just had to put away a thousand things to unearth his bed so he could lie down. Then I had to clean up his kitchen to find the sink to make him tea."

"Wait till you see how pretty Bea and Mr. Malachi and me made your kitchen for you!" Vivian called out, hopeful.

"And I," Mrs. Scott automatically corrected Viv's grammar. "Mr. Malachi and I." Then she sighed and looked back to me. "I see you fed and turned out the horses."

"Yes, ma'am."

"Do you know how to muck a stall?"

"Yes, ma'am."

"Really strip it?"

"Yes, ma'am."

"Well . . . I certainly don't have the money to add on another stable hand while Ralph is recuperating . . . and now there's Dr. Liburn's bill, which he deserves my paying quickly." She thought a moment, a moment of panic on her face as she clearly started ticking through all the other bills I knew she faced. "You proved today that you can ride in an open field on a steady, easygoing horse." She mulled that over. "That's not saying much."

Not saying much, I thought defensively. I wanted to tell her exactly how dangerous that ride had been. But it was clear she loved Charity, and hearing how the chestnut had plagued that mare would only make Mrs. Scott hate him more. I was beginning to see how fierce she was when someone she cared about got hurt. I took the criticism silently.

"Can you jump—truly?"

I thought of the bitty two-foot-high jumps Dandy Boy would hop over, me whooping and giggling. "Yes, ma'am. A little."

She studied me. "All right. Tomorrow let's see what you can handle in the ring."

I smiled.

She held up her pointer finger—a gesture I was learning was her sign for *hold your horses, don't get ahead of yourself.* "We'll see," she cautioned. "A horse *liking* you doesn't guarantee he will take a jump safely, or listen to you in a moment of doubt, or go through a whole course at a collected pace," her voice was getting weirdly quivery, "or won't dump you in a fit of insolence or . . ." Again, she stopped mid-thought. She straightened the small scarf she had knotted at her throat. "Tomorrow I will see if you know how to take a jump on a *sane* horse, not just a pet pony. Then, and only then, will I think through what is best—and safest—for everyone. If there's even a chance of training that cursed chestnut."

CHAPTER 15

"Heels down!"

I frowned. They were down.

Mrs. Scott walked to me and grabbed the back of my boot. "Like this." She tipped my heel back, so only the ball of my foot was in the stirrup-iron, my toes pointed up in a forty-five-degree angle.

"Toes in."

Ouch! I winced.

She stepped back. "Walk on."

I was on one of her dappled-grays, named Caspian. I had hoped for Charity, but Mrs. Scott said she was too old for jumping now. "Caspian's my truest jumper. If you can't take a small oxer fence on him, well . . ." She'd shrugged.

I tried to trust that Mrs. Scott was looking to help me prove myself capable by giving me Caspian for that first ride—even though he was enormous. Any fall from him was going to hurt—a lot.

That morning she'd come downstairs carrying jodhpurs and riding boots that pretty much fit me perfectly. Figuring they had once belonged to her daughter, I tried not to get the willies as I pulled them on, knowing something awful had happened between them over that chestnut. No matter how much I dismissed Viv's Ouija board, I had a fair dollop of superstition myself. It didn't help that Viv had pulled that dang thing out the night before to predict how I'd do in this test ride. *Uncertain* had been its answer.

Thanks a lot.

Caspian was a gentle giant, though. Knowing what was expected of him, he took himself to the fence line and walked the edge of the ring.

"Lengthen your spine."

I pulled myself tall.

"Shoulders back."

I squared them, like a soldier at attention.

Alarmed, Caspian threw his head up.

"Relax! If you are that stiff, you'll make him tighten up too."

Mistaking it for relaxing, I slumped.

"No, no. Sit tall, chin in, hold just a little hollow in your back."

I managed to comply.

"Better."

A compliment?

"Remember, a horse will only be balanced if you are balanced in the saddle. And balance is critical to jumping."

"Yes, ma'am," I murmured.

"Let's see if you know how to post a trot correctly. *Traw-aw-ot.*"

At the sound of her command, Caspian swung into an easy trot. I rose out of the saddle, up-down, up-down in rhythm with his movement.

After a few moments, she barked, "For pity's sake, get on the right diagonal!"

Confused, I bounced-bounced in the saddle, like children hop-skip to get their footsteps in sync, left-right-left-right, and then resumed my rise and fall.

"Stop," she called. "Whoaaaaaaa."

Caspian halted.

"Do you know what I mean by the diagonal?"

I hadn't heard that term before. Mama had just taught me to ride in the fields. Or maybe I just hadn't listened carefully enough—I was little then. Viv's age. But I fibbed, afraid to admit ignorance. "Yes, ma'am."

Mrs. Scott gave me that considering stare of hers. "The only way to improve, young lady—the only way I will work with a rider—is if I have complete honesty." She waited.

"I know to rise in rhythm with him as he trots forward," I squeaked, "so I am protecting his back."

"That's correct." Mrs. Scott softened the tiniest bit. "But things are more precise in the show ring. All about maneuvering a horse subtly and safely, in a way that augments his natural movement. So, in the ring, to post correctly, you must rise with his outside front leg, the one next to the fence. That's the correct diagonal. Understand?"

I nodded.

"Try again."

It took me a few bounces, but I found the right timing. Mrs. Scott watched me circle the ring twice before stopping me. "You are pushing off the stirrups with your feet, rather than just lifting your hips. So you are posting too high, hitting his back when you come back down, which is making your lower leg slip around."

That sounded awful. My heart sank.

She crossed her arms. "You need schooling without stirrups to develop a quiet seat."

I smiled. That implied a tomorrow.

She held up that pointer finger. "Let me see what you do with this little rail. It's low enough that you can trot over it. Circle wide and come to it straight on and centered."

I nodded, encouraged. *Tomorrow.*

But I got too excited—or too nervous maybe. I must have squeezed my legs too tight because

Caspian lifted into a canter, a beautiful surge with a reach to match his height. There was nothing mean-spirited about it. His was just a much bigger, longer, rolling stride than I had ever felt before. I swayed around with it and as he came to the tiny jump, I leaned way too far forward anticipating his leap.

He sailed over. Perfect. But I was already off balance as he left the ground and his rear end came up to arc over the rail. I felt myself pitch and vault right over Caspian's shoulder. I somersaulted in the air, then—WHUMP!—landed flat on my back in a cloud of sand, kicked up from my slamming into the ground.

I couldn't breathe—the wind knocked out of me as suddenly as if someone had clobbered me with a fence post. I gasped, gasped, gasped, like Mrs. Scott's dumb koi fish, trying to gulp in air. My heart pounded.

I heard hurrying steps. "Breathe," Mrs. Scott called. "Slowly. In-out."

Closing my eyes, I tried to calm myself enough to let my lungs work. But all I could think was *no-no-no-no, she's going to think I can't handle this.*

I considered just stopping trying to breathe.

A blast of hot air hit my face. Was this hell? My eyes popped open. There was a huge gray muzzle next to my nose.

"Give her room, fella." Mrs. Scott gently pushed Caspian away and dropped to her knees to look me up and down, anxious. Then she sat back on her heels. "Bravo, young lady. You didn't let go of the reins, so the horse didn't run off. That took presence of mind, which is half the battle in riding well. But . . ."

She helped me to my feet. Waited as I brushed myself off. Then, looking me in the eye, unblinking, she said, "That's that, isn't it?"

"What do you mean, that's that?" I knew my voice was too challenging, insubordinate even. One jump and I was done for?

"Young lady, Caspian took that fence sweet as can be. And you still came off. You're lucky you're not hurt. That fall wasn't Caspian's fault, was it?"

I shook my head. "But . . . but I just didn't have

the chance to get used to his canter stride. That's all it was." My despair gave way to mad. "You—you didn't give me time!"

Startled, she took a slight step back, a *how dare you* in her expression.

I didn't care. She was being unfair. And I was sick of unfair. "You—*you* said—complete honesty was the only way you would work with a rider. Well . . . yes, you're right, that wasn't Caspian's fault. But you—*you* didn't give me enough time," I repeated with a catch of a sob at the end.

Pursing her lips, Mrs. Scott twitched some sand with the toe of her boot before returning my glare. "You are correct. I did not." She paused. "Get back up on him and walk him quietly. So he knows you are not afraid of him. Which will keep him from being afraid of you. That is—if you wish to continue."

She was testing me. Squaring my shoulders, I walked Caspian to the mounting block, and swung myself back onto the huge horse. I'd been right, falling off him had felt like I'd been hurled out a second-story window. I willed my heart to stop banging nervously in my chest.

He sauntered peacefully back to the outside track.

After watching me walk the ring one full round, Mrs. Scott waved me over as she nodded to herself. I was recognizing that gesture of hers, too—it meant she had decided something in conversation with herself.

Please, please, please. I approached where she was leaning against the fence.

"Go round twice more, so he knows to listen to you even if I am not here. Then sponge him down and muck the stalls."

It was late morning now. The sun was high and starting to get hot. Shading her eyes, she assessed the sky, something she seemed to do a lot. "Still no clouds," she murmured, turning east-west-north-south. Then to me, she said, "Make sure you fill up the horses' buckets against this heat. But don't dump the water from yesterday. We need to conserve."

Wrestling the hose through the barn, I contemplated turning it on myself. Even in the stable's shade, it was boiling. By the time I dragged that heavy rubber pipeline all the way down to the chestnut's stall, I was lathered in sweat, encrusted with dirt, horrendously itchy.

He was neighing and carrying on, wanting fresh, cool water.

Bang! He kicked the wall.

"Hang on!" I called.

Bang!

"It's your own fault for being so cantankerous," I grumbled, "that you have to be all the way down the aisle, isolated from everyone else." I braced myself for his tantrum as I reached for the latch to his stall.

As I rolled his door back, though, he froze mid-gyration. Whickered at me. A horse's friendly *there you are* greeting.

Stunned, I whispered, "Hey, boy. Are you glad to see me? Me? Not just the hose?"

He bobbed his head. Answering me? Then, to

not be too agreeable, he kicked the wall, just a little, demanding his water.

"Okay, okay." I turned the nozzle to let water stream into his bucket, and he stuck his face in it, slurping deep, while swishing and splashing. He nearly drained the bucket as he played in it, even as the hose gushed a waterfall.

No wonder Mrs. Scott was so worried about rain. She'd said that her well had run dry two summers ago. How in the world did she keep the horses watered then? Did she have to haul it all the way from the creek?

I kept the tap open until the chestnut finally stopped, lifting his soaking wet muzzle and dousing my face with dribble as he rubbed his nose along my cheek and gently nibbled on my hair. I didn't move. Partially fearing he'd actually bite me if I moved, but mainly marveling at such tenderness coming from such a fearsome horse. He worked his mouth along my hair, just like I'd run my hands down his mane, scratching, to calm him down. The way pasture mates groom one another, helping winter coats shed out, getting rid of itches. I held my breath—it was such an act of acceptance. Of trust.

How I wish I trusted him enough—or my skills enough—to just get on him and start jumping. But the memory of hitting the ground hard from almost six feet up on Caspian kept that foolishness in check. I turned off the hose and put my face against his neck and patted him, whispering, "I'm going to get good for you, boy, as soon as possible. I promise."

CHAPTER 16

When I finally finished my stable chores, my body was smarting so much from my backflip and wrangling manure that I staggered up the hill to the house. I found Vivian sitting on the back stoop snapping the ends off a mess of string beans.

She dropped the colander, scattering her work on the grass and hugged me so tight, I almost cried. I was that sore.

"How'd you do? How'd you do?" She bounced

up and down on her toes.

"All right, I guess. Until I didn't. What have you been doing?"

"Helping Mr. Malachi. I picked these beans," she gestured to the ground. "Oh, shoot." She hastily swept them back into the pot. "And then he showed me how to gather eggs. The hens clucked all around my feet. It was such fun. Then I learned how to boil eggs. And Mr. Malachi taught me two French words: *poule* and *oeuf*. Hen and egg. He's promised to teach me more Frenchy-isms in case I ever make it to Paris. He fought in France, you know."

"Yes, I know."

"I made you a sandwich—all on my own! Mashed up eggs and butter. Come see."

I followed her inside to find the most squashed sandwich ever, her thumbprints deep in the soft bread.

"Ta-daaaaaaa!" She jubilated, holding out her hands.

I bit my lip to keep from laughing. "Why, Viv, that's a masterpiece. Thank you."

I started to sit down. I was so famished I didn't give a fig what the sandwich looked like. Besides, just two weeks before I was gladly eating cooked weeds.

"Oh no you don't, missy," Viv declared, putting her hands on her hips. "Go wash up first and make yourself presentable."

I could hear Mama's voice in hers so much it made my heart trip a beat. "Yes, ma'am," I play-acted along with her as I shed my dirty boots at the back door. "I'll be right back."

I tried to not think on how happy Vivian seemed and how much worse it would be now for her because of it if Mrs. Scott turned us away. For me too. Sudden anger welled up in me—despite my working so hard to not think on Daddy. How could he just leave us, without knowing for sure that we would be accepted and able to stay here?

In my socks, I slid silently along the hardwood floors to the staircase, passing Mrs. Scott's study. I honest to God didn't mean to eavesdrop this time, but I heard Mrs. Scott plain as day: "She's green. Unschooled. Last night I was thinking if she could ride well enough, that I could enter her and Caspian in the Warrenton Horse Show. Then, if he took her safely over the show's three-foot courses—going well for a young teen with no show experience—that I could then sell him to most anybody at a very good price. One of those New Yorkers with fat wallets, coming by train for the weekend, wanting a safe, reliable horse to hunt. A horse they themselves didn't have to train or even work out much. But . . . that was before she went tail over teakettle off Caspian. Over a nothing fence. I don't know that she has real jumping in her."

I had to clap my hand over my mouth to keep from shouting out another protest. She hadn't given me time! I felt myself moving away from the stairs to the study's door—to do what exactly? Interrupt and show how hot-headed I was, prove I was disrespectful? I forced myself to hold still and listen.

Thankfully, Mrs. Scott corrected herself almost as if she heard my thoughts. "But I hurried her. It's been a long while since I taught a youngster."

Now I did have to eavesdrop, to know what I might have to face next. I flattened myself to the wall and leaned toward the voices.

"You really want to sell Caspian?" That was Malachi.

"No. I never want to give up a horse that good and kind. But the property taxes are due. On top of the loan I had to take to get us through the drought two years ago. I must be pragmatic. And honestly, Malachi, I'm worried sick about the fact it hasn't rained. The corn has stopped growing. If I lose that crop again—like it withered without even tasseling two years ago—we're . . . we're done for. I don't think I could sweet-talk the bank into extending again. I'm not sure I could stomach doing it, either."

There was a long, long pause. The clock ticked. I imagined her staring out the window. "Now there's Ralph . . . and Dr. Liburn. He's only charging a few dollars—but that's all I've got to spare right now."

My face flushed hot with guilt. That bill was our doing, Viv and me.

A chair scraped along the floor, and I could hear Mrs. Scott get up and pace as she spoke. "That cursed chestnut has caused so much hurt and heartache. I'm hoping Ralph will heal, but he's . . . I don't want to admit it—nor does he—but he's old. That kind of injury is hard on ancient bones." She cursed the chestnut again. "At least the glue man's price will be something."

I gasped. Sending that beautiful horse to slaughter felt like a sin against creation.

"You don't think you could teach the girl to ride the chestnut?" Malachi asked. "You sure taught me to stick to a saddle."

"Oh, Malachi, you were a natural. The best steeplechase jockey I've ever seen."

"No, ma'am. It was because of the way you taught me, and your boys." Another pause. "I know you spent a mighty sum of cash to rescue that chestnut, Mrs. Scott. It'd be a terrible shame to not recoup it—like throwing a bucketful of money out the window. If you're thinking of going to the Warrenton show, with the goal of selling Caspian after he competes, you should think about this, Mrs. Scott—from everything you've told me, that chestnut is as gorgeous as he is wild. Perfect conformation, you said. Those monied hunt riders would love to possess that fancy a horse. If you can get him in line with a slip of a girl riding him, one of them will buy him for certain.

"And that sure would get you in everyone's mind again as the county's best horse trainer. Bring you lots of training work—if you want it. In addition to whatever prize money he'd win. You know he'd win—if that chestnut is as flashy as you say—the judges couldn't help but award him."

"Oh, he's that flashy."

Pressed against the wall, I nodded in agreement. He was that.

Malachi pushed on. "Vivian was chattering all day about how brave and smart her big sister is. She says with righteousness, 'My sister can do anything.'" He chuckled. "That little one's a pistol."

"They are sweet about one another," Mrs. Scott said. I could envision her pursing her lips and thinking. "But here's the thing, Malachi. That chestnut is a dirty stopper. It's not like a run-out refusal. You know that. It's hard for a seasoned rider to survive a dirty stop—that sudden brakes-on, shoulder-drop trick. If the young lady can't take even a teeny jump on Caspian—she could get hurt, seriously hurt, like . . ." A sigh. That loud ominous clock ticked. "Quiet hands and good instincts, though." Silence. "And gumption. The girl has lots of gumption, I'll give her that . . ." Mrs. Scott trailed off.

"Like Owen and Conroy?" Malachi's question was soft.

A long, long pause.

"Yes, like the twins."

"Well . . . they could tame and ride just about anything."

The clock ticked.

"I miss them, too, Mrs. Scott. Every day."

Her voice was halting and hoarse as she responded, "What concerns me is that the girl is more like Marjorie."

Another long, long, long silence.

When Mrs. Scott spoke again, her voice had returned to brusque. "No . . . I can't risk another chance on that horse. It's irresponsible to continue stubbornly hoping. The consequences of it being a mistake and going wrong again are too dire for . . . for whoever is on his back. The girl. She . . . she could break her neck from that kind of fall. No. I'll train Beatrice on Caspian. She can learn to jump a course with him—he is such a big-hearted schoolmaster. And selling Caspian at the show will get us through for a bit.

"But that chestnut has to go. I'll make the call in the morning. Can't be helped. Desperate times. Desperate measures."

CHAPTER 17

I didn't sleep at all that night.

How could Mrs. Scott be so cold? The feel of the chestnut's muzzle against my head, his nibbling my hair haunted me. He was just starting to trust again. To trust me. And he had gentleness in him. He did. He just needed it coaxed out of him. Mrs. Scott couldn't send him to slaughter. For glue and dog meat. I know it was desperate times. My whole life was desperate times. But . . . but she just couldn't.

Around four a.m., I thrashed out from under

the sheet, all clammy from sweat and balled up in worries. The night was almost as hot as the day had been. I went to sit by the wide-open window where there was a least a little breeze. Vivian murmured and rolled over. I quieted to make sure she dropped back off to sleep, remembering her racing into Mrs. Scott's study, crying out that Ralph was hurt, hurt bad—horror and guilt and fear all over her sweet face. I pulled in a sharp, shaky breath. That chestnut could have killed my little sister. My mind did a dirty stop of its own. Mrs. Scott was right. He wasn't safe. She should get rid of him—for everyone's sake.

And yet . . .

The chestnut liked me. I could tell.

If I learned everything Mrs. Scott could teach me, got really good as a rider, surely I could stick in the saddle for a course of jumps with him. Lord knows, he could jump any obstacle he wanted. He'd proven that. All he had to do was be willing to take me over them with him.

It was night—the time of dreams, undiluted by the brutal light of daytime realities. That FDR fellow was talking about a new chance. Why not me? And a horse that had been abused but somehow seemed to still have the ability to hope. To hope in me, anyway—that I would not misuse him. Didn't he deserve one, too? I just needed to show Mrs. Scott. Show her what I had experienced with him.

Slipping into those hand-me-down riding clothes, I tiptoed down the stairs to the beat of that loud hall clock. I was going to the stable. To get on that chestnut—come what may.

First, though, I was going to snoop. I wanted to look at the photo I'd noticed of Mrs. Scott's daughter. To take a good look at her face to see if I could figure out the mystery about this woman named Marjorie, so I could avoid being like her.

I turned on Mrs. Scott's desk lamp—ignoring the giveaway that light surely was. But I was so tired of adults knowing things I didn't. Their keeping secrets or making decisions about me without asking what I might think. Hints that the world was about to turn upside down because of adult foolishness, and children having no way to stop the disasters from happening.

Her bookshelves overflowed with framed photographs. I came to her boys first. Small on ponies. Then my age and a bit older—grinning, holding up ribbons and leaning on their horses, confident, clearly reveling in their victory, while not being surprised at all by it. About a dozen of those. A few serious-faced school portraits. One photo that had to be a young Malachi, in jockey silks, the twins' arms over his shoulders. Then finally, Mrs. Scott's sons in cavalry uniforms—standing tall beside war horses. Malachi said he missed them. They must have died in the war. I felt a wave of pity for Mrs. Scott. So much loss.

And what about her daughter? What had caused their rift, her refusal to talk to her mother? I wasn't so sure I would speak to Daddy if I ever saw him again. Was what happened with Mrs. Scott as hurtful as leaving a child behind in the middle of the night?

At the end of the long bookcase were photos of the woman who had been my mama's friend. There were only a handful. One as a truly beautiful baby. Another dressed in ridiculous frills standing beside a Maypole—about Viv's age. One of her in a gorgeous satin wedding dress with a train that had to be yards long, arranged in a swirl at her feet. A crown of pearls holding back wavy hair, a smile that was small so no Scott family dimples showing. She held a cascade of lilies, her other hand tucked in the arm of a handsome man, quite jaunty in his stance. And then the one I was looking for, her standing by that pony. I looked closely at that face. Her dimpled grin there seemed . . . *hmm* . . . forced somehow. I blew the dust off the glass and stared. More of a grimace, really, almost like . . . like she was afraid.

A small shiver ran through me.

I snapped the light off and marched myself outside into the predawn gloom.

There was just a hint of sunup, a thin red glow seeping along the earth as I came to the stable. The horses were still asleep—except for the chestnut. He was gazing out his stall's back window, away from the sunrise toward the dark, toward the mountains. If I were a poet, I could explain it better—but there was a *what-the-heck-will-this-darn-day-want-of-me* apprehension about him, a *bring-it* defensiveness. If a horse could have a proverbial chip on his shoulder, his was the size of a barn.

Somehow, seeing his angst, his desolation, in a moment all the other horses were sleeping blissfully—just like I had snuck out into the night, twitchy with disappointments and questions, while my sister and Mrs. Scott slumbered—made my heart ache. For him. For me. It's as if that horse embodied all the fury and fear and loneliness, the self-doubt and *what's-coming-next* anxiety I was feeling that morning. Heck—had felt every second since Daddy disappeared.

Hearing me approach, the chestnut swung around, pinned his ears back, and threw his head up and down threateningly—until he realized it was me. He went absolutely still then, pricked his ears forward, and nickered.

Stupid tears stung my eyes.

He nickered again, drawing me to him.

I held out my hands. He sniffed them, tickling my palm with that exploring upper lip horses do in greeting. And then he put his muzzle up against my head and rested there. I didn't move. He didn't either. We stayed like that for a long moment of wonderment for us both.

"Okay, boy," I whispered. "Here's your chance. Our chance. Please. Please trust me."

I went to the tack room to search for his bridle and saddle. They all had small bronze plates saying which belonged to which horse. Charity. Caspian. Cloud—that had to be the other dappled-gray. Hudson. Chesapeake. I guessed those were for the bays. Blue Moon. The coloring of roans is rare—so that one had to be his.

At last, I came to a bridle with a massive, heavy bit—long cheekpieces, a curb chain, and a twisted wire mouthpiece—a forceful bit meant to keep a fiery horse under control. The name plate: Vulcan.

Good grief! This gorgeous horse was named for the troll-like god of fire? The name suggested red coloring, of course. But geez.

Just like Viv had kept that Ouija board, I'd

stuffed Mama's *Bulfinch's Mythology* into my suitcase. Not as much for the Roman myths, but for its recounting of King Arthur's legends. Still, I knew the story on Vulcan was that he'd been born disfigured. His mother, Jupiter's wife, Juno, had been so displeased at the sight of him that instead of cradling him in her arms, she'd thrown him down—which on Mount Olympus meant a pretty far fall—and gave him an eternal limp. Making Vulcan notoriously ornery, forging weapons in a spew of red-hot sparks.

Talk about a horse's name becoming self-fulfilling prophecy!

When someone purchased a horse, especially a fancy one, his saddle and bridle were usually included, part of the deal, because they had been fitted to his body. Nameplate and all. But for pity's sake, why hadn't Mrs. Scott changed that name?

As soon as I thought on it, though, I knew why. Referring to him simply as "the chestnut" was detached, self-protective. It felt temporary. Easier to be rid of something that had no personalized name.

If I'd had any sense, even if the name Vulcan didn't make me hesitate, that gargantuan bridle bit should have stopped me in my tracks.

But it's a fact that when a body doesn't sleep, a person isn't entirely right in the head. All sorts of nonsense can roll around up there. Like thinking you can tame a dragon that has already laid waste to a whole town. Yanking the intimidating bridle off its hook and grabbing a saddle with the same nameplate, I toddled under their weight back to the chestnut's stall.

I expected him to kick or bite when I came toward him with that big and nasty bit—I would—but he took the cold, harsh metal into his mouth without a fuss. The saddle pad and saddle, too. But the girth—when I tried to cinch up that soft fleece-lined belt—that's when he lost it.

The chestnut spun and knocked me against the stall's wall, neighing frantically, pawing the stall's bedding so hard that shavings flew up into the air around me.

"Whoa, whoa now," I managed to croak. "It's all right."

He reared, landed, and tossed his head in that aggressive, snaking motion wild horses do to warn off attackers.

"Eeeea-sy. I won't hurt you." I needed to get that saddle off him. He'd hurled me to the side before I could tighten the girth, so the saddle was starting to slide down along his rib cage. If it slipped completely underneath him, to hang from his belly, any horse, even Charity, would have a fit that would only endanger him and me more.

"Eeeea-sy, eeea-sy." I stepped forward and got my hand on the billets and quick yanked them up, releasing one side of the girth as the chestnut shied away from me, reared again, flipping the saddle off and up to the rafters and then—*THUMP!*—to the ground, those stirrup irons just missing my head.

As soon as it was off him, he simmered down, then stood, trembling.

"It's all right." I gently ran my hands along his neck and chest. "All right." He flinched when my hands reached his side. Snorting, he eyed me suspiciously.

Of course. Those scars. The girth must have

rubbed against those scars. Keeping my hands quiet, I stroked his side, saying, "I won't hurt you, boy. I promise."

Slowly, he stopped quaking.

Well . . . Mrs. Scott said I should school without stirrups. I took the bridle's reins in my hand and walked the chestnut to the ring.

I refused to think. The arena was filling with the sunrise's rosy haze, still low, making the air all around me pink and hopeful, flush with the promise of a new day, a new deal. Witnessing the world resurrecting itself from the night, rising up with such beauty and reassurance, filled me with faith, a willingness to dare anything. To not be timid, just as that FDR man had said.

"Trust me, boy," I murmured as we reached the mounting block. "Eeeeea-sy."

Would I be able to get on him without the footing of a stirrup to lift myself up and onto his back? I climbed to the block's third step. He wasn't as tall as Caspian. It was his attitude that made him seem gargantuan. If he didn't spook or rear or bolt, in theory I could get on. Standing on that highest step, I was basically parallel to his back.

"Eeeeeeea-sy." I put the reins over his head, gripped them, and grabbed mane. "Stand," I crooned, "stand."

He didn't move.

Please, Mama. Help me now. Holding my breath, I slid onto his back, taking my feet from the safety of the mounting block.

He quivered.

I let my legs dangle loose, fearing that tightening them against his side would spark the same volcanic reaction as the girth. Of course, without gripping my legs, if he took off at that moment, I'd hurtle to the sand.

Please, Mama.

He jigged a little in place, shook his head a bit, then brought himself to a standstill, one ear forward, the other back. Listening, waiting to see what came next.

I had no idea.

"Beatrice."

At first, I was convinced I was hearing Mama. I caught my breath. The chestnut's ears twitched forward, back, forward.

"Don't try anything else." It was Mrs. Scott. Speaking low and soft, almost a whisper. Once more she'd appeared like a watchful cat emerging from shadows. "Just let him get used to your sitting on him. Remain very still."

I didn't turn to look at her. She didn't move forward. We were suspended in the magic of the chestnut accepting me on his back. He seemed to marvel at it, too.

Three, maybe five whole minutes passed, as the sun rose higher and higher, warming my face, its golden rays making his red coat coppery.

Only then did the chestnut stamp his foot with some impatience.

"Slide off him now and give him big praise."

I didn't want to leave our communion, but I knew Mrs. Scott was right—it's always best to quit a riding session on a success.

Slipping to the ground, I threw my arms around his neck. "Good boy." He tucked his muzzle into the crook of my neck.

"Well, young lady," Mrs. Scott's voice was still soft. "That was nothing short of a miracle."

I turned and she was approaching us slowly, carefully, to not spook the chestnut, to stand where she and I could face one another.

"Why no saddle?"

"You said no stirrups." That was plain old dumb sass on my part. I don't know why I said it.

She raised an eyebrow. "If you got up on that horse thinking you'd ride him bareback because I said work with no stirrups on Caspian, I would think you far too foolish to school."

I bit my lip. Honesty. Mrs. Scott required it. And isn't that what I ached for too—for adults to respect me enough to be straight with me? "He seemed afraid of the girth. Those scars."

She nodded to herself. And then, talk about a miracle, she smiled—slight, but enough to show a dimple. "Looks like you have a horse to train."

CHAPTER 18

I still had to spend the morning on Caspian. Not that he wasn't a lovely ride. And I knew that's the way of it with horses—a rider must walk before she runs, so to speak.

"The faster you improve, the sooner we can put you on the chestnut," Mrs. Scott had said. "And we're on a bit of a fast track here, young lady. A month until the show. It is insanity. But," she shrugged, "are you willing to be pushed?"

"Yes, ma'am."

"All right, then." To begin, she instructed me to

stand in the stirrups for a few moments, the iron bar under the ball of my feet, pushing my heels down as far as I could, until my calves stretched out, long and taut. "Now, lower your backside into the saddle slowly, not moving your legs. That will show you what heels down should feel like as you ride."

The tendons in the back of my calves burned.

Of course, that was nothing compared to the twenty minutes of riding without stirrups to teach me the feel of a seat with a grip. My thigh muscles were on fire as I kept my legs bent, my calves in the hollow behind Caspian's shoulder blades, my heels clasping his belly.

"Relax your knees and ankles," Mrs. Scott shouted as we cantered around the ring. "You should feel bowlegged."

Finally, she let me come down to a walk and dangle my legs to ease the cramping. "Good. We'll do that every day for the next two weeks until I see no air between your bottom and the saddle."

Oh joy, I thought with an inward groan.

But joy did come—at the end of that session,

Caspian and I took that bitty jump perfectly. Then another, slightly higher, then two, one after another.

"Well done," said Mrs. Scott. "Come see me after you muck." She turned and walked up the hill, searching the vivid-blue, cloudless sky as she went.

When I hobbled to the house for lunch—muttering, "I love riding, I love horses," against my legs' screaming soreness—Dr. Liburn was there. He'd checked on Ralph and come to report to Mrs. Scott that the stubborn stable hand would only heal if he stayed still. The doctor had found Ralph out in his tomato patch, trying to weed with his good hand, cursing.

She'd left in a huff to fuss at Ralph.

"God help him," Dr. Liburn had said with a laugh, watching her go.

"He better hope she doesn't tie him to a chair to keep him still," Malachi joked. "Would you like a cup of coffee before you continue your rounds, Doc?"

"I would," he answered, settling into a chair. "I have things to talk with you about as well."

"I'll get it!" Viv hopped up and went to the stove, where a steel coffee pot sat on the stove. I rushed forward to strike the match to light the flame for her, so she didn't burn herself, but she waved me off. "I know how! Let me do it, Bea."

"She's getting handy around here," said Malachi. He turned his head in my direction. "And I hear you snake-charmed that mad-hatter chestnut this morning."

I smiled. That meant Mrs. Scott had been talking about me.

"What's this?" Dr. Liburn asked.

"Got up on that horse that near killed Ralph," Malachi answered. "Stood sweet and quiet for her, Mrs. Scott says."

Dr. Liburn let out a low whistle. "Be careful, though, Beatrice. That horse packs a mean punch. I don't want to be splinting you up, too."

"Yes, sir," I murmured.

Proudly, Vivian brought the doctor a steaming cup, and he blew on the coffee to cool it before pulling some papers from his pocket. "I went to that FDR rally, Malachi. Next one I should take you. I was inspired. Truly moved." The doctor looked at Viv and then me. "A young woman, a Miss Falligant—a lawyer herself—led it. Let that give you girls some dreams." He dropped one of the papers on the table and took a long sip.

It was a campaign flyer. There was a photograph of FDR—a pleasant-enough looking man—and big headlines: *He's Ready! Are You? We Need Action! The fundamental cause of our distress has not been remedied. Conditions demand Roosevelt and a New Deal.*

He pushed another flyer forward across the tabletop—this one of a farm auction. "Please read this aloud for Malachi," he asked me. "As I finish this," he looked to Vivian, "tasty cup of coffee. I need to be on my way soon."

I read:

THE FARM:
BEST HOME OF THE FAMILY.

FOUNDATION OF CIVILIZED SOCIETY.

AUCTION: Sixty-acre farm, twenty-five miles from Washington, between Lincoln and Unison. Never-failing stream running through entire farm. Fifty acres tillable land, balance timber. Five acres of fruit—apples, peaches, pears, cherries, plums. Stables, dairy and stock barn. Farmhouse with six rooms and indoor bath. Level ground for alfalfa, corn, wheat, oats, potatoes, beans, and cabbage. Extra-good well of water. All livestock, machinery, tools, and furnishings.

"Who is it this time?" Malachi asked.

"Old Berryman's place."

"The Quakers? Oh no," Malachi shook his head in disbelief.

Dr. Liburn drained his coffee and stood. "At the rally, some people were talking about organizing a penny auction. And I am trying to help spread the word."

"What's a penny auction?" Malachi asked.

"A new way that farmers are trying to stop bank foreclosures. When the auction gavels in, people shout out laughably low bids. A nickel for a cow. A dime for a plow. A penny for a chicken. But everyone must be in on it, so everyone else stays quiet. That way the single bid stands. The bank is forced to accept it. After the auction is over, neighbors can give everything back to the farmer since all they spent might be a quarter. Think some of your mama's people would come?"

Malachi nodded. "I can arrange that. I know Mrs. Scott would come, too."

"Good." Dr. Liburn put his hand on Malachi's shoulder and cautioned, "It has to stay secret until the day of, though. And watch your back, Malachi. Bankers are fighting these penny auctions tooth and nail. But the hope is that if enough penny auctions happen around the country, it will convince banks to extend loans to give farmers more time to make their payments—until the economy improves. Gives the bankers a chance to act human."

I caught Vivian's eye. I could tell she was thinking about our father, the banker. Once upon a lifetime ago, Daddy had talked about how much he enjoyed helping a family buy a house—their own home—for the very first time. People used to smile—genuinely—and tip their hats to him in greeting as we passed on the street. That was before bankers became so despised.

For a moment, my mind wandered along the roads, wondering where Daddy was. If he was all right. Then I shifted to puzzling on how Daddy could go from a man who helped others with such commitment to someone who couldn't even help himself. Or his own daughters. The terrible responsibilities he had shoveled onto me, as heavy as the manure I dumped in the wheelbarrow.

I felt Viv watching me. I slammed the door on my imaginings and feelings to keep her from seeing them, how sick to my stomach I felt. If she did, she might ask again where I thought Daddy might find a job, when he would come back to get us. And I wasn't sure I could manage to keep up the ruse for her this time.

When Mrs. Scott came back, she was all agitated about Ralph. "That man. Honestly. He's stubborn as ten mules put together. I'm going to have to check on him every day to make sure he doesn't do more harm to himself." She shot a withering look at Viv and me—her glare obvious as to whom she blamed for Ralph's condition. She cloaked it before Vivian noticed. But I saw it and felt the heavy weight of the trouble that we—total strangers Mrs. Scott owed nothing to—had caused her and the people she cared about.

"Malachi," she continued, "can you and Vivian gather extra eggs, please. Then devil them. I'll take those plus some ham and biscuits to Ralph tonight. To keep him away from his stove."

"Yes, ma'am." Malachi took Vivian's hand.

After the screen door slammed behind them, Mrs. Scott turned to me. I couldn't read her face. Was she going to backtrack on what she said to me this morning? After I'd proven myself? I felt my chin jut up in defiance and self-righteous outrage, no matter my sensible side warning me to not worry a wasp nest.

Pouring herself some of Vivian's coffee, she gestured for me to sit as she took a sip. But Mrs.

Scott grimaced, turned her back, and spat back into her cup what she'd almost swallowed. "Lord have mercy," she mumbled and put the cup into the sink.

She leaned against it to face me. "Seeing again how injured Ralph is, I really need your father's permission to teach you on a horse that is potentially so dangerous."

Not this again. Not now. I shook my head.

"If you truly don't know where he would go to look for work, I must ask the sheriff to make enquiries. I don't have the right to make that kind of decision about your safety. We are not family."

Family? The word cut me open. The way she said it contained all the promise of family—parents' being responsible for a child's safety. Protecting them. As if that were reality, I thought with a ferocious bitterness that frightened me. A hundred demons suddenly flooded out of the cage I'd locked them in. I shook my head harder.

"I am afraid this is not your choice, young lady."

Not my choice? Since when had I been able to

decide anything? All I'd been able to do was try to deal with whatever circumstances I was shoved into. "Not my choice?" I screeched, my tone shocking me as much as it did Mrs. Scott. "Nothing has been my choice! None of this—this Depression, my mama dying, my daddy selling off everything, my being here." I frenetically shook my head, just like a dog does when it's been stung by a bee.

"Young lady, calm yourself. I—"

"Calm myself?" I shouted. "You don't understand. My father wouldn't care."

"Oh, pshaw," her voice softened. "Of course he would."

"He doesn't! He just left us in the hayloft in the middle of the night, without saying goodbye, expecting you to take us in. For me to convince you to . . . to . . . !"

Mrs. Scott cocked her head. "He did what?"

"He left a letter. He—" I started to sob. "A letter. A letter and Mama's . . . Mama's . . ." I choked.

Mrs. Scott took a step toward me in sympathy, but I staggered back from her. "A letter. A letter."

I was making no sense. I couldn't explain it with words. "I . . . I'll show you." I felt myself running, scrambling up the stairs, blindly yanking open the drawer where I had hidden the handkerchief with Mama's locket and ring and the photograph of the four of us and that awful, awful, world-ending note.

Stumbling back into the kitchen, I threw it onto the kitchen table, like it was a hot poker out of a blacksmith's fire. "Read it!" I cried.

But before she could, I recited the lines that I had read in disbelief a hundred times over, "*Tell her you are Cora's girls. I'm sure she will take you in and take good care of you, the way I cannot now.*" I sobbed. "He left us—like unwanted babies on the stoop of an orphanage."

The screen door slammed.

I whirled around.

There stood Vivian, her sweet face pinched with hurt. "You told me he was coming back," she whispered.

I hadn't. I hadn't told that lie. But I had let her

believe her assumption, her hope. “Viv,” I murmured, “I’m so sorry. Daddy—”

But before I could get anything else out, Vivian bolted, as pell-mell and as whipped up with shocked and disappointed fury as the chestnut.

CHAPTER 19

"Viv, wait!" I cried, scrambling to run after her, struggling against the soreness in my thighs that made me slow.

"Get away from me!" she shouted over her shoulder. "You lied! You said he was coming back."

"Viv, I didn't, I—"

"Leave me alone!"

"Viv!" But she had already sprinted beyond hearing me. I'd never seen her run that fast. She was halfway down the long driveway leading to the main road. Where was she going?

The lane twisted and went up and down in little ripples of hills. She disappeared around one of those turns. When I got to it, I couldn't see Vivian. Anywhere. "Viv!" I shouted. Turned around, shouted again, cupping my hands to my mouth. "Viiiiiiiiiv!"

A bunch of crows took off from treetops, annoyed with my disturbance, *caw, caw, caw.*

Then silence.

I kept running until I reached the county road. Looked left, looked right. Nothing.

"Viiiiiiiiii-viii-aaaan!" I called again. *Please oh please, Viv. Don't you leave me.*

I heard the splutter and rattle of Mrs. Scott's truck coming up the lane. Malachi was with her.

"Get in!"

We drove along the road about half a mile, turned around and went the other direction. Nothing. We repeated it, slower, with my standing in the flatbed, so I could see farther. Still nothing.

"Maybe she cut across the fields," Malachi said, "and got down by the creek."

Mrs. Scott considered a moment. "We can't drive the truck over the pastures." She motioned for me to get into the cab, turned back down her lane, and drove so fast, Malachi and I both bounced hard enough that we had to put our hands up against the cabin ceiling to keep our heads from hitting it.

We lurched to a halt down by the stable. "We need to split up. Malachi, you stay here in case that child doubles back. Maybe check the henhouse and the gardens in case she eluded us and slipped back here to hide somewhere. That's what the boys did the one time they announced they were running away from home. Just about her age when they did that." A pause. "Young lady, tack up Charity. And I," she muttered as she opened her door and slipped to the ground, "I will take Cloud."

Malachi looked toward Mrs. Scott's exit, astonishment on his face. "Well, I'll be darned." He elbowed me. "Scoot now to keep up. And don't worry, we'll find Vivian." He climbed out, murmuring to himself, "If that don't beat all."

Mrs. Scott tacked up twice as fast as I did, the process obviously as natural to her as breathing. Then she swung up onto Cloud as graceful as a ballet dancer.

"I'll head in the direction of town," she said. "You go the opposite way. Circle back in an hour if you haven't found her. It'll be dusk then. Can't ride in open fields after that. You won't see holes that could break a horse's leg." Mrs. Scott caught the despair that clutched me as she said *dusk*. "We'll find her before that, I'm sure. Keep to a walk or trot. If you canter, you might just pass your sister too quickly to notice her." Mrs. Scott clucked at Cloud and rode off, so fluid and connected to him, their silhouette as she reached a hilltop looked how I'd always imagined a mythological centaur appeared.

Charity and I rode toward the creek. "Viv!" I shouted over and over, Charity's ears twitching back and forth with my calls. But she didn't spook. "VI-VI-AN!"

Nothing.

I walked Charity up the creek for a long way. With no rain, its water was lower than the previous week, so it was easy to keep to the creek bed.

"VIV!" I shouted and shouted and shouted until the shadows were growing so long I knew I had to turn back.

Each *clop-clop* of Charity's hooves as we headed toward the stable felt like a drum beat of doom. Vivian could get hurt out here in the darkness. She'd be afraid. I went back and forth between cursing Daddy and cursing myself. Should I have shown her his note? Would it have been better for her to have known from the get-go? How was I supposed to know these things?

Mrs. Scott was standing by the paddock, watching for me. I saw her nodding to herself as I approached.

"Beatrice," she said quietly, reaching out to hold Charity still for me to dismount, "now I must call the sheriff, so he can help us look for your sister and get word to other jurisdictions in case she manages to get herself to Leesburg or elsewhere."

This time I nodded as well. "Yes, ma'am." All I cared about at that moment was getting Viv back.

"I'll wait until you come up to the house to place the call, so you can describe her."

Quickly, I untacked Charity, brushed off her sweat, and hurried to the house—numb, no longer thinking.

As I reached the door, I noticed the strangest thing bobbing along the lane. A small light. *Oh my God.* I panicked again. "Mrs. Scott!" My voice cracked from all the shouting for Viv and from a new, terrified foreboding. Didn't the angel of death carry a lantern?

She came to the door. "What in the world?" she muttered, coming out onto the stoop with me.

We realized at the same moment: a bicycle lamp. *Thank God. Just a bicycle!* It reached the circle in front of the house, and a boy's voice called out, "Hello in the house!"

Balancing on the crossbar, and hanging on for dear life, was Vivian.

I barely heard any of the conversation as I

rushed toward my sister. She had twigs in hair, her dress was torn, and her knees were bloody. But she was found—in one piece.

"She was up in a tree and fell to the ground just as I was passing on my way here," the boy was saying. "Grandpop sent me to make sure—now don't be blaming me for what he said, Mrs. Scott—to make sure the horses weren't standing knee-deep in manure without him."

"Viv, are you all right?" I tried to wrap my arms around her. But she turned her face away from me and dropped off the bike to her feet.

"Viv, let me help you."

She limped to the house. All she'd let me do was follow.

Vivian refused supper. Refused to let me bandage her knees after she soaked in the tub. Refused to speak. She slipped into bed and pulled the sheet over her head.

I sat at her feet, keeping watch. I don't know

from what danger. Me maybe?

The full moon rose, bathing the room in silvery, ethereal light. That downstairs clock ticked the minutes away, but time for me, in that room, just stopped passing.

Finally—hours later?—there came a soft knock on the door. Mrs. Scott slipped in. Putting Daddy's handkerchief and Mama's precious belongings onto the night table, she sat on the other bed facing me. "Parents sometimes do the absolute worst, most foolish things," she whispered, "thinking they are doing what's best for their children." She looked at me solemnly as she spoke those words, a moonbeam lighting up her face, revealing—for just a moment—a face awash in sorrow.

"I don't know your father. But I remember your mother. Very well. She was my daughter's best friend in college. Cora was here often during school breaks." Mrs. Scott took in a small, shuddering breath before murmuring, "It was a lively place back then." She paused. "Your mother was delightful. Bubbly. Affectionate. Smart. An excellent rider. Beautiful in the saddle. Brave, but never reckless. Horses trusted her. She was a very good influence on my daughter. A true friend."

Mrs. Scott looked down to something in her hands. "It took me awhile to find these. Two photographs of your mother when she was only a few years older than you are. About eighteen, I think."

Standing, she held out the photographs for me to take, putting her other hand on my shoulder. "I hope when your sister wakes up tomorrow, she will want to stay. After all, you and I have horses to train and compete at the Warrenton show. Including that blankety-blank chestnut. He's responding to you the way I witnessed horses responding to your mother. They—to use your word—*liked* her." Mrs. Scott nodded, thoughtful. "I am sorry for the reason and the way your father did it, Beatrice. But I am glad he brought you here to me."

Then she glided out.

Tomorrow. It was now promised.

I held the photographs up so I could see them

in the moonlight. Mama in show attire, standing next to a white horse bedecked with ribbons. Smiling, her hand caught mid-stroke on the horse's muzzle, quieting him, in that soothing way she had. How many times had I seen her pick up Vivian when she was a toddler, crying in dismay over something she couldn't possibly understand at that young of an age—Mama's mere touch calming her and bringing a chortle from my little sister. Suddenly, I could hear the silly songs Mama sang to us both. *Bubbly.* That was a good word for her.

The other image was of Mama and Mrs. Scott's daughter, arm in arm. It was closer-up, so I could really see Mama's face, looking amused by something. Luminous and loving eyes, soft curls, easy smile, heart-shaped face. I felt my eyes well up and quickly held the photograph away so my tears wouldn't ruin it.

"Is that Mama?"

I startled at the sound of Vivian's voice. She crawled over to me, lifted my arm, snuggled underneath its crook, and gazed at the images.

"See how much you look like her?" I whispered.

I felt Vivian shrug, sad. "I don't remember her looking like this."

"Oh gosh, Viv." I hugged her. "That's how Mama looked before she got sick. She was such fun." As I said it, I realized, really recognized, how little time Vivian had had with our mother. She was barely six years old when Mama died. The parent she knew—the one who had defined for her what being parented offered—was Daddy.

"I . . ." Her voice was so pained, so soft, I had to listen hard to get what she said next. "I am afraid of forgetting Mama altogether."

"Oh no, honey. No, no. I won't let that happen." I started talking, sharing stories of Mama. "She used to make up treasure hunts for us," I began, "leaving notes with hints and riddles around the house to lead us to a hidden present. We built little houses out of mud and moss in the garden for fairies. And . . ." Memories poured out of me—of happy, whimsical times, of our home and family before it all changed, before the world fell apart, taking us with it. Memories I hadn't dared to take out and look at for a long, long time.

And as I felt Viv nod with each little anecdote, I clung to them myself, holding onto the remembrance of what life could be, of what being safe, of what love—steadfast, unblinking, unequivocal—had felt like.

CHAPTER 20

For days, Vivian stayed mournful quiet. All she would say about Daddy was that maybe he was like the fireflies, shining against the dark, then disappearing, eventually to return again. I let it go. What else could I say anyway?

She stayed away from the stable, shadowing Malachi as he did his chores. At twilight, she even took to walking him to the cottage where he lived that was just over a hill and a few acres distant from Mrs. Scott's house, asking that he tell her more Frenchy-isms as they went. Then she sat on the porch swing with me, saying she planned to go to France as soon as possible, reciting phrases over and over—*merci . . . je m'appelle Vivian . . . le soleil est chaud aujourd'hui*—while launching the swing into such a huge, angry arc that my stomach lurched.

For me, the week passed in a blur of heels down, no stirrups, cantering Caspian in wide figure-eights. Mrs. Scott was teaching me how to get him to yield and bend from my leg—instead of steering by the reins—and to not cut corners in the ring when approaching a jump. "If he's swerving and leaning as he heads into a fence, he's not balanced. He's more likely to clip the top rail and knock it down. In the show ring, that will cost you points," Mrs. Scott explained.

She explained a lot.

"Get him collected! You want his strides between fences to be the same."

"Leg on, leg on! Don't let him get slow and all strung out!"

"Don't choke him! Release the reins a little as he goes over a jump, so he can extend his neck."

"Get your bottom off his back as he vaults!"

"Don't look down as he lands! Look up! Look to your next fence so he knows where you're taking him."

She was a firehose of information. And always, always came the warning when I fumbled: "If you do that on the chestnut, he'll give you trouble."

She'd said she was going to push me. But until I experienced it, there was no way of knowing just how demanding, how unrelenting Mrs. Scott would be. By the end of the week, she'd worked me so hard, I felt like I might have to put my hands to my legs to pull them forward step by step—that's how sore I was.

Mrs. Scott showed absolutely no sympathy about it, either. And no mercy in her training. If anything, she just pushed me harder as she saw me improve.

Sometimes when she made me repeat a combination Caspian and I had just done perfectly or barked at me to correct some infinitesimal boo-boo, I wanted to scream back at her, calling her all sorts of bad names. Or to throw my riding helmet at her head. Or to run her over with Caspian.

But . . . at the end of all that torture, I got to ride a full course—ten fences, one after another, snaking around the ring. Oh, it was like flying as we cleared each of those jumps—gliding through air for those heart-stopping, laugh-out-loud-in-delight moments. Mrs. Scott had raised the poles in height little by little, from inches above the ground to two feet, to two-six, without my noticing. So I didn't get anxious about the increase. She'd only inform me of the change after I went over without a clip or a stumble.

She'd even shouted: "Bravo!" Three whole times.

That's when I finally dared to ask, "Can we try the chestnut now?"

Mrs. Scott pursed her lips, thought, nodded to herself. "Yes. Soon."

Then—as she always did after making a pronouncement—she left, shading her eyes to search the sky.

Tantalizing clouds. But still no rain—not a drop.

The next morning, I went to the stable before sunrise, to continue my courtship of the chestnut. I'd been getting there early to brush him before tacking up Caspian—talking to him, running my hands along his belly and those scars to get him less fearful of my touch. He no longer flinched and shied away, so I had started putting the saddle on and taking it off him, tightening the girth a little bit more each day. Not so tight that the saddle was secure enough to ride in. But getting there.

As horrible sore as I was, I almost skipped down the hill—like Vivian in one of her joyful cavorts—I was so excited. *Soon.* How soon was soon? Today? Tomorrow? The day after that? Preoccupied with that riddle, I didn't hear the *schwoop-thunk* until I was at the stable's entrance.

Happy days are here again! The skies above are clear again.

I caught my breath. "Mr. Ralph?" He couldn't be well enough yet to be back to work. "You better quit," I called, "before Mrs. Scott sees you!"

A head popped up in Caspian's stall. "But Mrs. Scott knows I'm here." It was the bicycle boy!

"You! What are you doing here?"

"Mucking."

"But . . . why?"

The boy lifted his cap and pushed back his hair. It was already hot enough, even at predawn, for his thick mop of dark hair to be plastered with sweat. He took a deep breath to load up before reciting: "Grandpop said that Mrs. Scott said to him that you were doing serious training now. And Grandpop said, that being the case, that you needed some help with the mucking to keep from wearing out, seeings how you're just a girl, after all." He grinned and winked—just like Ralph did—a disarmingly blue-gray eye.

I sort of wanted to ball my hand into a fist and punch him. "I'm perfectly capable of doing the mucking!" I went for the other pitchfork and marched into Charity's stall.

Schwoop-thunk. I chucked a pile of her dung into the wheelbarrow sitting in the aisle, half full already from the boy's efforts. Oh lord, how my legs protested the movement.

"Suit yourself." *Schwoop-thunk.* "But Grandpop said to tell you—if you wanted to cut off your nose to spite your face and not accept my help—to remember that handling the chestnut is going to take all your concentration and strong—not exhausted—legs."

Schwoop—I stopped mid-muck. "Wait. What?"

Thunk. The boy dumped his pitchfork and came out of his stall to push the wheelbarrow to the compost pile. He was about my age, tall, lean, and gangly. His resemblance to Ralph was striking. I could now see the good-looking teen Ralph must have been once upon a time and a thousand wrinkles ago—which made me blush somehow. I shook off that weirdness to listen to him.

"Grandpop said that when Mrs. Scott checked on him last night, that she told him that she was going to keep you working Caspian, so she could enter you and him in the Warrenton show. But she also said that you were now ready for her to try you out on the chestnut—to see what was possible."

"Really?"

"Yup."

"When?"

"Today."

I gasped. "Today!" My heart leaped. "Today?" I think I danced a little.

The boy laughed. "Boy oh boy. Grandpop sure does know you people. He said to tell you—if you got all excited—to whoaaaaaa down. Mrs. Scott plans to try you at the walk. That's it for now. But Grandpop also said to tell you: to show Mrs. Scott what you got. And that if you had any sense at all, that you'd just say thank you," he gestured to himself, "to me for the help."

He leaned over and started to put his hands on the wheelbarrow's handles. "Oh," the boy straightened up. "Grandpop also said to tell you that Mrs. Scott got spooked bad about the chestnut. So she might be more protective of you than you need. And that she'd probably show her concern by being high-handed and prickly, and that you should pay it no never mind. Aaaaaand . . . that you might just need to push back on Mrs.

Scott a little bit yourself to get her comfortable with the idea of you being on that hellion horse. Grandpop said that Mrs. Scott told him that you had gumption. He says to be sure and show it."

The boy rolled the wheelbarrow forward. "Oh, right, one more thing." He stopped. "Grandpop said I was to mind my manners and introduce myself to the nice young lady. My name's Rex—which means 'king,' if you didn't know. Nice to meet you." Then he pushed on, singing: *Let us sing a song of cheer again. Happy days are here again!*

Show Mrs. Scott what I got?

"Wait!" I called, running to catch up.

I knew exactly how the bicycle boy could help me. He could hold the chestnut as I cinched up his saddle's girth and got on. I just couldn't wait any longer! I wanted to *show* Mrs. Scott that I was ready to not just walk, but to go, go, go!—the instant she came down for the morning's lesson.

It ended up being far more peaceable than I had anticipated. The girth. Climbing the mounting block. Putting my foot into the stirrup and swinging into the saddle. The chestnut was calm through it all. All my painstakingly quiet, careful coaxing and grooming had been worth the trouble.

Now, though, came untried territory.

"You sure about this?" Rex asked, still holding onto the bridle, looking up at me—in the middle of a wide-open ring, with plenty of space for a rebellious, fiery horse to work himself up into a deadly tornado.

I didn't know Rex at all, but I could see he was nervous for me. I gathered up the reins. Nodded. "Let go."

As Rex stepped back, the chestnut swished his tail—loud, like snapping a flag, puffed up in horse-swagger. Pranced in place. Threw his head up and down.

My heart pounded, knocking against my chest. "Easy. Easy, boy. We're all right." I patted his neck, hoping he couldn't feel how much my hand was trembling. "Stand." He kept tossing his head and mane but started to quiet a little. "Staaaaand."

Only when he stood absolutely still—his ears

pricked forward, ready to listen to me—and only then, did I give him the go-ahead. "Walk on."

Oh my.

Malachi was right. That chestnut was fancy. I'd never before felt a horse move like that. It wasn't a mere walk. He sashayed, he strutted. I laughed out loud in delight.

I couldn't help it—I wanted to see what his trot was like. "Traw-aw-ot."

He lifted into a jaunty, two-beat bob. Steady, fluid, not jarring at all. I grinned and found myself sitting his trot easily, swaying with him.

As the sun rose, a red, glorious fireball spilling its light into the arena, I felt him wanting to go faster. Holding himself back, respectful of my not having yet asked, but still chomping at the bit. Not out of pent-up rage for once. He seemed to truly be enjoying himself. So I let him pick up speed. The chestnut was just too beautiful a mover to stop.

He rolled into a lovely, loping, lilting canter. Once around the ring. Twice. I cut across the arena diagonally and then—during the canter's moment when all four hooves are off the ground as a horse literally sails into the next stride, suspended like a bird in midair—I felt an extra little lift, like a single beat of wings, before his back hoof struck ground again.

A flying change.

The balletic moment a horse switches his lead leg, allowing a new direction, mid-flight.

Something a horse usually won't do under saddle, unless his rider has a light seat and soft hands, the two are in perfect sync, and he is happy in the partnership, willing to make the rider's choices his.

Tears of astonishment filled my eyes. I turned to call out to Rex, "Did you see that?"

Standing next to him in the middle of the ring, arms crossed, a scowl on her face that could ignite a hundred thunderstorms, was Mrs. Scott. She pointed to the ground in front of her. Her hand-command for me to stop. Right now. And to come to her. Just like Mr. Ralph had said, high-handed and prickly.

CHAPTER 21

"Don't ever ride that horse without my being present." Mrs. Scott's voice was low, shaky. "Ever. Do you understand me?"

"But—"

"Ever."

I frowned. "Did you see how—"

"I did."

I slid off. "Good boy," I murmured, patting the chestnut, angry disappointment boiling up in me. What was her problem? Impertinence was clearly all over my expression when I looked at her because her eyebrow shot up sky high.

"Ever," she repeated.

I glared at her. She glared right back—for so long Rex started fidgeting and the chestnut stamping his hoof.

"Rex, please take the chestnut and give him a good rubdown and several carrots as a reward," Mrs. Scott instructed. "He did well."

What about me? I fumed. If she thought the horse did well, then what in tarnation was going on in her imperious, contrary mind? I think I might have even stamped my foot, just like the chestnut.

Mrs. Scott held up that dictatorial pointer finger. "Not ever," she repeated, reaching out to put her hand on my shoulder.

I shook it off.

And then, I still can't believe it—she laughed. A genuine, mirthful chuckle. "Good lord," she said. "Gumption, all right." Then she sobered. "That's the kind of stunt your mother might have pulled. Aided and cheered on by my boys. But, Beatrice, that horse is not safe. Not yet."

My glare eased a little.

"Think of it this way. Be practical. A good horsewoman—a true equestrian—is always practical. And I get the sense you want to be one. Yes?"

I nodded.

"All right, then. Listen carefully. That was an absolutely lovely ride." I started to speak, but that pointer finger of hers went up again. "But it might not have been. Rex is not a trainer. He wouldn't have known what to do if that horse acted up on you." She paused to make sure I was absorbing her words. "And if you get hurt—or the chestnut gets injured because you couldn't handle him—then neither of you can show at Warrenton."

My mouth popped open.

"Yes. If you two go that beautifully, you two will win every class you enter." She nodded in her way, mostly to herself, deciding.

The chestnut and I were going to show!

"And I need you to do that for me, Beatrice," she said quietly. "To win your classes." She sighed and rubbed her forehead, then pushed her glasses farther back on her head, to pull her hair away from her face. "Everything could depend on that show now," she murmured.

I suddenly noticed that her eyes were red and swollen. Had she been crying? Was that possible with her? Then I realized she was in her going-to-town outfit.

"The corn is ruined. Parched and dead. Yet again. Because of this drought. I need to speak to the bank. I wasn't going to take you with me, but . . ." she trailed off for a moment. "I think it's time for me to start spreading the word a bit about your riding my horses. Start the rumor mill. Gossip—around here anyway—is a very effective way to stir up interest in horses before they enter a ring. And you seem to read people well." She nodded, squared her shoulders. "Please go on up to the house and get changed."

"Millicent!" Mr. Craig, the grocer, spotted us on the street and hurried his robust self over to shake her hand. "And howdy-do to you, little lady," he patted my head. "You look much improved since I last saw you, sweetie, some peach in those cheeks now."

I held my tongue and smiled dutifully, ignoring the greeting more suited to a five-year-old.

"Speaking of peaches, Milly," he began.

"They were fine specimens, weren't they, Curtis."

"Of course. I expect only the best from you."

She kept the banter going. "The best is what you deserve."

"I'm wondering if you might be bringing in some corn later this month?" Mr. Craig turned serious. "This drought. Terrible. I'm having trouble finding vegetables to stock. Everything around here is scorched."

Mrs. Scott shook her head. Lowering her voice, she said, "That's actually why I am here, Curtis. I've lost every stalk. Withered before the cobs had a chance to grow. I'm hoping the bank will grant me an extension into October. Beatrice," she gestured toward me, "is helping train some of my horses. To show at Warrenton and maybe sell to some visiting Long Islanders as they come down for the hunt season. I just need a little time."

There was my cue. "Mrs. Scott's a mighty fine trainer," I piped up. "I barely knew anything about riding before, and she's got me jumping. Great big horses. Normally I would be scared to death. But her horses are all so sweet and agreeable and good to me. They just pop over those fences, taking me with them." I smiled—my eyes big and innocent. "Easy-peasy."

"She's even up on that chestnut," Mrs. Scott added. "You know the one."

For a flash, Mr. Craig looked shocked. "Well, now, isn't that something." He grinned at me and leaned in to whisper conspiratorially, "There's no better horsewoman around here. You're a lucky little girl to be learning at Millicent's knee."

"Yes, sir." I nodded.

Mrs. Scott smiled, flashing her dimples, as Mr. Craig looked back at her. "Shame about your corn, Milly. Be forewarned, I've heard the bank's been flooded with similar requests all week. This drought is looking to be as bad as the one two years ago." He shook his head. "Of all times to be hit with no rain again—back-to-back."

Mrs. Scott stiffened. "How bad is it?"

"Honestly?" He frowned. "I don't think anybody's going to have any corn or hay, from what I'm hearing. And there's talk that apples are going to be stunted and half the size of what they usually are come October. All the pickers are panicking, 'cause no one is hiring. Lord knows how they'll get by." He sighed. "County employees are going to be hurting too. The board of supervisors just had to cut salaries fifteen percent—teachers included, and they are barely paid as it is. I'm extending credit at the store as much as I can, but . . ." he trailed off. "After a point, I can't, or I'll go under."

Mrs. Scott put her hand on his arm. "You're a good man, Curtis."

They stayed frozen like that for a moment. Then Mr. Craig attempted to be jovial, patting his fulsome belly. "That and my good looks will get me by, I suppose."

Mrs. Scott slipped her hand through his arm and squeezed it a little. "Always has, Curtis, ever since grade school."

He smiled, bolstered.

Pulling away, Mrs. Scott returned to brusque. "Wish me luck. Come along, Beatrice."

And we crossed the street to the bank.

Inside the bank, Mrs. Scott left me sitting in a row of wooden chairs as she conferred with a man in a stunningly crisp, three-piece linen suit and bow tie, his hair carefully parted and slicked in place. Seated below a huge propeller ceiling fan, behind a massive mahogany desk, he seemed totally impervious to the heat that was wilting everyone else. He was so picture-perfect and groomed, he made my skin crawl a little. But he was nodding, listening, deferential, as Mrs. Scott talked.

Then he spoke, pushing papers around on his desk, until I saw Mrs. Scott put her hand to her heart. She bowed her head slightly before she stood, shook his hand, and came toward me, her face as still and fixed as a statue, like she was holding her breath. Or holding back vomit.

I followed her into the street. Only then did she visibly exhale. "Eight weeks," she murmured. Putting her hand on one of the elm trees lining the town's main avenue, she stood stock-still, recollecting herself. Her being so visibly shaken made me feel all sorts of nervous—Mrs. Scott always seemed so strong and certain of herself. Irritatingly so, but still, somehow that lent a sense of stability. I looked away down the street to let her get over her upset, without my staring at her.

A knot of children had gathered in front of a big white building with a scallop-shaped front, decorated with balloons. I craned my neck a bit to see what that was about and could read a lit-up sign: The Hollywood Theater.

Mrs. Scott followed my gaze. "Ah, she's opened it, then," Mrs. Scott muttered, a brittle edge to her voice, even more so than usual. "I hear that movie house has three-hundred-and-fifty cushioned seats. And is air-cooled, somehow."

Did the town even have three-hundred-fifty

people? "Who is she?" My curiosity got the better of me.

"Evelyn Corker. The heiress bride. Two years ago, after the crash, her groom still had the cash to purchase a beautiful, historic home Lafayette himself visited when he came back to the United States after the Revolution. The family living in it had been there for forever—but these are hard times. So many people I grew up with are close to destitute and having to sell, to outsiders mainly. Evelyn's husband bought that grand old estate for her as a wedding present—lock, stock, and barrel plus two thousand acres."

I was surprised by the details Mrs. Scott was sharing. She was usually a lot terser. I could tell this woman got under her skin.

"They're the ones Ralph was talking about building that enormous horseshoe stable. They've added a flying field, of all things, to come and go to New York by private plane. And a racecourse to train thoroughbreds for the track." Mrs. Scott paused. "But . . . she's an accomplished show rider herself. I'll give her that."

A willowy woman emerged from the theater's front door.

"And there she is." Mrs. Scott straightened up, talking more to herself than to me now. "Yes . . . quite a good rider, in fact." She nodded. "And she likes grays. Come along, Beatrice."

Briskly, we walked the brick sidewalk to the theater, Mrs. Scott plastering on a sparkling smile before calling out, warm and friendly, like a purring cat, "Congratulations, Evelyn. The theater looks beautiful."

An absolutely stunning woman, with a face and chic aura I'd only seen before in magazine ads, turned to us. "Mrs. Scott, how nice to see you. I hope you're coming to see *Tarzan*?" She gestured to an illustrated poster of a man in leopard skin battling a lion with a knife. Thirty cents a ticket, fifteen for children, and a quarter for matinees. The woman frowned slightly as she eyed me and then did a quick glance at Mrs. Scott, taking in our obviously way-out-of-date attire. It was quick, but I saw it. And I know Mrs. Scott did as well, because I could feel her ice over as the theater owner added, "Of course, if you bring some tomatoes or beans or homemade apple butter or the like to Friday matinees, we are letting people in for free. I'm sending the donations to the local Red Cross. There seems to be a terrible malnutrition problem among some of the county children, poor lambs."

Mrs. Corker turned to me. "Do you like the movies, sweetie?"

What was it about people in this town thinking I was a dumb-kid sweetie? I was thirteen-going-on-fourteen, for pity's sake. But I swallowed my indignation. "Yes ma'am, I do. But to be honest?" I knew why Mrs. Scott had approached this woman—it wasn't about the moving pictures. "I like horses better."

"Well, goodness!" Her voice carried that syrupy lilt some people use for dogs and little children. "I do too. Isn't it such fun?"

"Yes, ma'am. Mrs. Scott is teaching me to jump on the prettiest dappled-gray you've ever seen." I think I may have batted my eyelashes at her.

Not missing a beat, Mrs. Scott demurred,

"Well, Caspian's an agreeable soul. Beautiful conformation and coloring, too. Much like that dappled-gray hunter of yours, Evelyn, that you showed in the spring at Upperville. I have a pair of them—Caspian and Cloud. Beatrice is progressing so quickly I'm going to enter them in the Warrenton Show"—she leaned in toward the theater lady to whisper as if I couldn't hear—"but, of course, I could put a toddler on Caspian, he is such a trustworthy schoolmaster."

Mrs. Corker smiled. "I had forgotten what a renowned trainer you are in these parts, Mrs. Scott. When we first came, I was told that I should seek you out, that you had an excellent eye for horses."

Mrs. Scott smiled back. "How kind of whoever told you that."

"You know, I have a few new horses that I'm deciding what to do with. I'd love your opinion of them. I'm heading home now. Might you have time for a little look-see and perhaps some tea? I'd love to know you better. I've been so busy with all the improvements to the estate, I've been terribly remiss in chatting up my neighbors." Her tone was socialite smooth.

With a dramatic pause, Mrs. Scott checked her wristwatch, seemed to do some figuring in her head, and said, "Why, yes. We have a smidgeon of time before my next appointment. Do you mind if Beatrice accompanies me?"

"Of course!" Mrs. Corker turned to me. "I have a lovely litter of Great Dane puppies you can play with, sweetie pie."

CHAPTER 22

Belching and rattling, Mrs. Scott's truck followed the theater lady's sleek Bentley up a long driveway, thickly graveled and flanked by young hickory trees. I noticed Mrs. Scott's grip on the wheel was turning her knuckles white. "Well done in town, young lady. You are becoming quite a good foil for me. Now . . . dealing in horses requires knowing as much as possible about potential buyers as well as the animals. Evelyn and her hubby? Money out their ears. They throw outrageously lavish parties—backgammon gambling, boxing matches to entertain guests, thirty-piece orchestras, tamed monkeys to pet. A year ago, they even offered a five-thousand-dollar prize for the winner of a foxhounds meet they hosted."

"What?" I blurted with incredulity. I couldn't fathom a five-thousand-dollar prize to begin with—and for dogs? That was the amount Daddy said he'd paid for our home—our lovely three-bedroom brick house with flowers and a lily pond and our backyard paddock and two-stall barn. The home we'd had to give up.

Mrs. Scott glanced over at me. "I know," she said. "But . . . despite that, they seem decent enough. For instance, last time Mr. Tucker came by with our milk—he's had to let his driver go and is delivering his family's dairy products himself these days—he told me he'd pulled in here on his buckboard, lugged his five-gallon cans onto that rather palatial white-columned porch, and knocked on the front door. An English butler opened. Told Mr. Tucker in the haughtiest of accents to go to the back door delivery entrance. Then slammed the door in Mr. Tucker's face."

Mrs. Scott almost laughed again. "Well, there's no way Mr. Tucker would brook that. He pounded on the front door and informed the manservant—loudly—that he had never gone to a back door in his life and wasn't about to begin now.

"Evidently Evelyn's husband heard the commotion and came to the front hall. He apologized for the butler's rudeness, invited Mr. Tucker in for coffee, and after a pleasant conversation said that in the future, Mr. Tucker could leave the milk wherever he wished, even atop the piano if he liked."

Mrs. Scott nodded. "So there is hope for this couple. If we carry ourselves with dignity, and don't become defensive, they will likely respond in kind. Remember that—no matter how intimidating the surroundings. All right?"

"Yes, ma'am." I thought about how intimidating Mrs. Scott's house had been at first—even as weedy and in need of paint as it was.

With one final, loud backfire of exhaust, Mrs. Scott parked the truck on a grand circular driveway in front of the gigantic horseshoe-shaped stable. I tried not to gape.

Filling the inner courtyard of the U-shaped barn were boxwood hedges and flowerbeds that bloomed with geraniums and marigolds—despite the killer drought that had fried Mrs. Scott's cornfields. A good two dozen immaculately groomed horses gazed out their stall windows at the beautiful gardens.

Mrs. Corker ushered us in, saying, "The horse I'd love your opinion on, Mrs. Scott, is in the back."

We passed a paneled tack room with leather armchairs; a laundry for saddle pads and blankets; a dressing room; an office; a medicine dispensary; tiled wash-stalls with hot and cold water spickets; and a small kitchen for preparing hot bran mashes for the horses. A groom, wearing starched khaki pants and a pressed white shirt with a fancy seal stitched into its breast pocket, brought out a gorgeous bay thoroughbred, perfect in her proportions, with those long, lissome legs that give the breed such speed.

"I know mares rarely win races," Mrs. Corker began, "but I am hopeful about her. Or perhaps I'll use her for hunter shows—I'm just not certain she is A-circuit material." She instructed the groom to trot the mare out so Mrs. Scott could assess her.

Inside a small ring, the man began jogging alongside the horse, clucking his tongue to keep her moving at a good pace.

Mrs. Scott watched. Six times around. "Other lead now, please," she asked.

I marveled at the mare's grace—she was as floaty and nimble as the chestnut. Absolute perfection. Oh, I had to swallow back a sea surge of awful jealousy. To have such a horse—and likely two dozen just as wonderful from the looks of it. Jeepers.

"She's off," Mrs. Scott said quietly.

I couldn't help shooting her a look of disbelief. What was Mrs. Scott trying to do? That mare didn't look a bit lame to me.

"You can bring her to a walk now, please," she said to the groom, "and then to a halt." Mrs. Scott approached the mare, whispering something to her as she gently ran her hand down the horse's front legs to her hooves. "She has a bowed tendon, right here," Mrs. Scott stopped halfway down, just beneath the knee, along the cannon bone. She felt the other leg. "Here too. Size of a baby dried pea, but definitely there."

Mrs. Scott straightened back up. "She just needs a little time to recuperate and heal. And then start back to work slowly. She won't be able to race on the flat now. But she could likely be a lovely jumper with the right training." She turned to face the heiress. "But," Mrs. Scott smiled, "you knew that already, didn't you?"

Putting her hand to her hip, Mrs. Corker burst out in tinkling, mischievous laughter. "I did. Several much-ballyhooed horse traders totally missed it, though. Including the one who sold her to me. Or . . . so he says. But that's the danger in the horse business, isn't it? *Caveat emptor.* Buyer beware and check the goods carefully yourself. That mare has heart—she hides the injury well. But I certainly won't be dealing with that trainer again. I can't be certain of him now, and honesty is everything to me."

Mrs. Scott shot a quick, *see-what-I-mean* look at me.

Mrs. Corker cocked her head. "Tea?"

"I'd be delighted," Mrs. Scott answered.

"Bob, please put the mare back in her stall and show—" The lady gestured toward me. "I'm so sorry, sweetie, what's your name again?"

"Beatrice."

"Please show Miss Beatrice the kennels. I know she'll just love meeting Bessie and her pups."

When Mrs. Scott reemerged from the house, I was knee deep in puppies—which, I must admit, were pretty swell. Bessie gave me one last sloppy kiss as I exited the kennel, watching Mrs. Scott approach.

She was arm-in-arm with Mrs. Corker, who was laughing and laughing. "Oh, I would have given anything to see that, Mrs. Scott."

"He rolled right off into the biggest mud puddle you've ever seen," Mrs. Scott concluded whatever story she was sharing, "still holding that chalice up high—without spilling a drop."

"Oh, oh, oh." Mrs. Corker had a hand on her side. "I've laughed so hard, my ribs ache."

I stared at Mrs. Scott—she should be an actress. Or was chatty and friendly her real personality and the more withdrawn, scary one the result of all the troubles and loss and money worries she'd endured? Suddenly, I felt the oddest urge to hug her.

"We'll transport the mare to you tomorrow. I'm so glad we happened upon one another in town, Mrs. Scott." The heiress kissed Mrs. Scott on both cheeks—or near them, because I could hear the *schmackkk* hitting air. "And don't forget about next Saturday. Seven o'clock. Formal attire, of course. All the men will be in their hunt colors." Then she waved at me. "Bye, bye, sweetie. Come see the puppies again soon!"

We climbed into the truck and drove away with a belch of smoky exhaust.

"She's sending you that mare?" I asked with some excitement. I was getting greedy.

Not until we reached the main road did Mrs. Scott answer. "Yes, for training, after she has rested for a bit. Evelyn isn't going to pay me anything—honest to God, these rich people can be so tight with their money when it comes to paying others for their work and expertise. But we have a little wager, she and I, that could help me a great deal. If I win."

"What's the wager?"

"That I can eventually get the mare jumping three-nine fences, four feet in spread, and triple bars to five feet. Without pulling a rail. By spring, for the Upperville show. It's the nation's oldest show—held each year since 1853. Quite the social event. Very much Evelyn's style. The first step toward qualifying for the National Horse Show as well.

"It's a gamble, though. I don't even know if the mare *can* jump. But we'll see. Nothing ventured, nothing gained. And I just wanted to . . ." Mrs. Scott trailed off for a moment, re-scrutinizing something in her mind. "I suspect someone was working that horse on a lunge line in too tight of a circle. Probably happened before the mare got to her, but—"

The truck backfired, interrupting, and Mrs. Scott said no more as she turned onto a road I didn't recognize.

"Aren't we heading—" I stopped and gulped. I'd almost said *home.* I shook my head to get rid of that ridiculous, that pitiful hopeful, that completely unjustified thought that I could call Mrs. Scott's house *home.* I felt the joy of that afternoon go flying out the truck's open window. I better watch myself, I thought.

"No, we're heading to a foreclosure auction Malachi told me about." Mrs. Scott glanced at me and then back to the road. "You all right, young lady?"

"Yes, ma'am," I mumbled, and turned to stare at the passing scenery.

I could feel Mrs. Scott eyeing me again. But I stayed silent. And she let it alone.

CHAPTER 23

We pulled into a wide-open pasture near a rangy red barn, edged by a large crowd. Farmers mostly, white and Black talking together earnestly, wearing their work overalls, worn, dusty boots, and sweat-stained wide-brimmed hats. They'd clearly left their chores to walk across fields or drive wagons to the auction. Their burly horses stood placidly, glad to rest, stamping to rid themselves of flies swarming their thick legs.

Across the sun-burned grasses, at a considerable distance from the farmers, were a handful of men in linen pants and jackets, bright-polished shoes, their neatly shaven faces shaded by dapper straw boaters. They leaned nonchalantly against gleaming-clean cars. The tall, crisply tailored, picture-perfect banker was with them. And parked alongside that column of wealthy gentlemen was the man I had so feared meeting—the sheriff. He held a shotgun.

"Oh no," Mrs. Scott muttered as she turned off the truck. "Malachi was hoping the hunt set wouldn't come. They certainly won't keep to the penny bid concept. They'll be after the land." She got out quickly and strode toward Malachi. I hurried along behind.

I swear I could smell the tension and resentment growing among the farmers as we slid through the crowd. Looking around them, I located my sister, Dr. Liburn, and Malachi. The doctor seemed his usual engaging self. On his lapel he wore a big round pin—for FDR, I imagined—and he was handing out flyers to people. Malachi had his head cocked, listening to conversations around him, his expression apprehensive.

Vivian—oh poor Viv—looked stricken. My stomach lurched. My little sister always wore her heart on her sleeve, in to-the-bone honesty. Seeing her expression unleashed a hailstorm of horrible memories—of the day my family's world was dissolved and sold off to strangers. Obviously, such recollections were pounding her as well.

When I reached her, Viv hurled herself forward and clung to me. We stayed wrapped together—amid a sea of men about to witness what we had experienced as children—being stripped of belongings, of home, of self-definition, of any sense of safe harbor.

Snippets of comments swirled around us.

A man who looked like he could lift a bull off the ground totally on his own was saying, "What the heck is wrong with the bank? Old Berryman is good for his debts. He's a Quaker, for pity's sake. They never cheat anybody."

"Well," whispered his neighbor, "he's missed two interest payments—last fall and this spring. Almost three hundred dollars total. He planned to make it up with bumper crops this summer. But this heat and dry spell have killed that hope."

"What's left on the mortgage itself?"

"It's bad—a little over two thousand dollars."

Nearby someone else whistled, low and long. "That much?"

I thought back to the five-thousand-dollar prize awarded hounds for running down—faster than other packs of dogs—a beautiful wild fox.

Another man, thickly muscled from a life of hoeing and hauling, spoke up. "You know, I heard Old Berryman offered to give stock in his farm as payment for the back interest. Betting on future growing seasons being better. Bank turned him down. Didn't understand that's the way it is with farmland. One year's god-awful. You make it up the next."

Murmured agreement. "Ain't that the truth." "You just have to have faith." "And elbow grease."

Something about the last exchange seemed to goose Mrs. Scott. "Excuse me, did you say Mr. Berryman offered investment stock in his farm as settlement on his current interest debt?"

"Yes, ma'am." The farmer looked sheepish for

being caught gossiping and tipped his hat at her. "That's what I heard."

I looked up at her, Vivian's arms still around my waist. "What does that mean, Mrs. Scott?"

She glanced down at me and seemed to startle a bit at the sight of Vivian clinging to me so tightly. "It means the bank would become a partner with Mr. Berryman. A stockholder in his farm—not just the owner of his loan. That way the bank would always receive income going forward—like dividends—from the farm's success, not just interest payments during the loan's short term. It means trusting the farmer to do everything humanly possible to turn a profit again and standing by him until he does. Honestly, it's far better for the bank, besides being more humane. Especially in this Depression, which came about through no fault of these farmers." She put her hand on Vivian's head. "Are you all right, child?"

Vivian buried her head even more against my side. Before I could explain, the auctioneer stepped up onto a wagon.

"Gather round, folks." He cupped his hands to

bellow. "We're about to begin."

The sheriff strode forward as well to stand beside the wagon.

Malachi called into the crowd, "Remember what we talked about. Stay the course."

The farmers around him nodded, their jaws set. The sheriff craned his neck to see who'd shouted.

The first thing offered was a mare—a lovely, quiet, well-formed ebony mare with four white stockings stretching up her legs. An elderly farmer, dressed in his Sunday best, led her to stand by the wagon. Mr. Berryman, I supposed. She nudged him fondly, and he smoothed her mane, his lips moving, obviously talking low to reassure her. He kept his gaze downward, toward the ground, too embarrassed to look up at his neighbors.

I heard Mrs. Scott groan at his conspicuous, heartbreaking sadness. "I know that brood mare," she murmured. "She's dropped several lovely jumpers. Sweet-natured and willing, just like she is. Oh, what a shame. She's never known another home."

Tears stung my eyes. Just like Dandy Boy, I

thought with a pinch at my heart.

Reading off his clipboard, the auctioneer announced, "Eleven-year-old mare, completely sound except for an accidental wire cut to her hock from loose fencing. Foals well." Then he began his snare-drum-quick cry: "What am I offered? What am I offered? Do I hear a bid?"

The farmers around me remained silent. Stubborn.

"Come on, folks. What am I offered? What am I offered?"

The sheriff took a step toward the crowd. The farmers seemed to inch forward to square off with him.

Looking around at the intensifying standoff, Dr. Liburn took in a deep breath and shouted: "Fifty cents!"

The rich, straw-boater men guffawed.

"What? Why this mare's worth three hundred times that, folks," called the auctioneer. "Do I hear fifty *dollars*? A fifty, a fifty?"

"Don't bid anything else," Malachi said loudly,

and his instructions rippled through the group, farmer to farmer.

The banker walked to the sheriff and pointed toward Malachi, clearly identifying him as a potential troublemaker. The lawman raised his gun, holding it across his chest, and kept his gaze trained on us.

Mrs. Scott frowned. "This is going to get out of hand," she muttered.

"I'll give you ten dollars for the mare!" One of the boater-hat gentlemen shouted, waving his arm.

As one, the farmers swung their heads round to glare at the gleaming-car contingent.

"A ten to the gentleman." The auctioneer bowed momentarily and began his chant again, "Do I hear twenty? A twenty, a twenty, a twenty?"

No one moved.

"Going once, going twice—"

"Fifteen dollars!" Dr. Liburn shouted.

"Doc! You don't have that kind of spare cash," Malachi protested.

"Fifteen! I have fifteen," the auctioneer brayed.

"Do I hear twenty, a twenty, a twenty?"

The boater-hat man waved his hand again.

"Twenty! Thank you, sir." The auctioneer pointed at the rich bidder. "Now . . . do I hear thirty? A thirty, a thirty, a thirty?"

The penny auction concept was derailing. Mr. Berryman pressed his face into the mare's mane. I could see his shoulders shake.

Vivian raised her head. "What will happen to the horse, Bea? Will she be all right? Do . . . do you know what happened to Dandy Boy?"

That's when I could no longer fight back tears. Ashamed of my lack of composure, I sob-whispered, "No. I don't know. He . . . he could be anywhere . . . with anyone."

Hearing me, Mrs. Scott exploded with a rather unrefined word before putting her hand on my shoulder to steady me. Then she reached over to tug on the sleeve of the farmer who seemed to know the farm's specific debt. "Sir, you said Mr. Berryman had missed close to three hundred dollars in interest payments. Do you know the exact amount?"

The man gaped at her.

"Quickly, man!"

The auctioneer called, "Twenty! Going once . . ."

"Two hundred and forty-two dollars," piped in another farmer standing next to him. "I'm a Berryman cousin. I know for sure."

"Twenty! Going twice . . ."

"Mrs. Scott, no, don't—" Malachi cried.

But Mrs. Scott nodded and swam through the crowd to its front. "Two hundred and forty-two dollars!" she shouted.

The crowd gasped. The auctioneer stopped mid-shout, his mouth hanging open.

Marching herself to the picture-perfect banker, Mrs. Scott spoke quietly to him, his head bowed down to hear her. After a few moments of listening, the banker escorted her with pronounced courtliness to Mr. Berryman. The two of them conferred for a long time with the old farmer, who stroked his mare's neck as if his life depended on it as they talked.

No one else moved or spoke—not even a

whisper—watching, waiting, astonishment hanging in the hot air.

Finally, the banker turned toward the crowd and announced: "This auction is concluded!"

A stunned cheer rose from the farmers. The boater-hat gentlemen shook their heads and got into their cars. Although I noticed one looked toward Mrs. Scott, an appreciative grin on his face, before he climbed into his maroon Packard and motored past us, its Flying Lady hood ornament glinting in the scorching sun.

Mrs. Scott remained talking with Mr. Berryman.

None of the farmers moved, not an inch, until she shook Mr. Berryman's hand, then the banker's, and walked back to us, head held high—her expression changing with each step—from victorious to rebellious to momentary self-doubt and at last to her signature mask of marble-statue-still resolve. I had watched her face enough to read it now.

The crowd parted for her, each one of those farmers removing his hat in reverence as Mrs. Scott passed by him.

"Come along, Beatrice. Vivian." She took Malachi's arm and said in a quiet voice, "Well, I've done it now, I suppose. But . . . because my bid covered Mr. Berryman's back-owed interest payments, the bank agreed to end the auction and let his loan stand. Took a bit of sweet-talking, though. I could negotiate that only when Mr. Berryman agreed to build coupes along his fence line for the hunt to jump and granted them unrestricted access to ride across his acres—which placated the banker, since he's such an avid foxhunter himself."

"Do you get the mare?" Malachi asked.

"No," Mrs. Scott answered, "I asked for stock in his farm instead and the promise of the mare's next foal. She's carrying now."

"But where are you getting—"

"That two hundred and forty-two dollars? The bank folded it into my note."

"Oh, Mrs. Scott." Malachi sighed. "How in the world will you cover that additional debt?"

"We'll do well at the horse show." She nodded her head. "Sell Caspian at the highest price possible. And Beatrice and the chestnut wow everyone."

I fell in line behind her as we walked to the truck.

"Well, young lady, you agreed to my pushing you as a rider. Now it begins in earnest."

CHAPTER 24

Every day at dawn, I rode the chestnut, trying not to panic about how much was now—to make a really sorry joke—riding on me.

At first, a long lunge line coiled in one hand, Mrs. Scott walked the width of the ring, following us as the chestnut cantered. I knew why. She was keeping abreast of us to safeguard me if something went wrong—but honestly it made me nervous. The expression on her face, too. Like I imagined a sentry on a fort wall, anticipating a barbarian enemy to come thundering in at any moment.

What did Mrs. Scott think she was going to do if the chestnut decided to take off on me? Lasso and reel him in? I'm not sure a strong man would be able to stop him anyway, and she was, well, I don't know how old, but she wasn't exactly young.

But the chestnut didn't take off on me. Not even a hint of it. He pranced. He floated. He radiated joy in every movement. Even during annoying conditioning exercises, like trotting over cavalletti ground polls. His delight made me forget the pressure on us. I even had to bite my lip sometimes to keep from laughing aloud in glee.

Finally, Mrs. Scott stopped shadowing us and set up a little crossbar. "Before you go over this, recount what you have learned about taking a jump."

I sighed. Really? Hadn't I been jumping Caspian beautifully each day over three-foot fences?

Raising an eyebrow, Mrs. Scott reminded, "This horse has a dirty stop in him. You need to ride well to keep him from doing that. You've coaxed him into trusting you. But I don't trust him yet—nor should you. He's not a big-hearted packer like Caspian." She crossed her arms, waiting.

Inwardly rolling my eyes, I recited: "A jump has five phases: the approach, takeoff, suspension, landing, and departure. I need to ride all five equally well. In the approach, it's my job to help the horse prepare by gathering him into a balanced gait with even tempo and stride, and then find my line and the right takeoff point in front of the fence. In takeoff, the horse shifts his entire weight into his hind haunches to shoot himself up and into the air. As he lifts off, I need to get my butt off his back, crouch forward so my spine is holding the same arc as his, so he is free to stretch his neck for better balance and tuck his legs up under him to sail clean over the fence. As he touches down and departs, I need to sit back and regather the reins to help him recollect into a steady canter to head to the next fence."

She nodded. "Go ahead, then."

The chestnut loped over the teeny obstacle. We circled and took it again. And once more.

From there we moved quickly. We had to. I could almost hear that eerie hall clock in her house ticking down the minutes to the horse show.

Mrs. Scott set up a mini course of four two-foot-high fences. When we took the first, I caught my breath at the force and height of the chestnut's takeoff, the surge of power from his back legs. We landed, cantered easily, and soared over the next three. Triumphant, I slowed and trotted back to Mrs. Scott.

Applause erupted at the gate. Rex was clapping and whistling, the manure wheelbarrow beside him.

"We are not in need of commentary from the fence line, young sir," Mrs. Scott called to him, shading her eyes against the brightening sun.

Grinning, he pushed the wheelbarrow away toward the manure pile.

Mrs. Scott patted the chestnut's neck, looking up at me, a hint of a smile on her face. "Methinks the boy has a bit of a crush." She held up her pointer finger as I felt myself blush like sunrise. "Don't get distracted. Now, those jumps felt different from Caspian's, didn't they?"

"Yes, ma'am! I mean . . . I love Caspian. But to

compare them? Hmm . . . Caspian skims closer to the top rail and lands sooner."

"Yes, that's right. Caspian's jump is more efficient," said Mrs. Scott. "Easier to ride. This chestnut is what show judges call 'scopey.' More athletic and arced, higher loft, bigger clearance of the jump. He will be able to take much higher fences than Caspian."

"Oh yes, ma'am," I blurted. "I've already seen him jump four-, maybe five-foot-high obstacles." Without thinking, I spilled the story that before I'd had the good sense to keep to myself. "When you sent me after him on Charity, after he hurt . . ." I started to stumble right there, foolishly reminding her about the chestnut kicking Ralph. No turning back now, though. My words raced out to get past that mistake. "I saw him jump all sorts of stone walls back and forth as he charged around after Charity. He was—"

Mrs. Scott reached out and put her hand on the toe of my boot. "This horse went after Charity?"

Oh no. My mouth popped open. Closed. "It . . . it wasn't mean-spirited, Mrs. Scott. I think he was just trying to play with her."

She studied me in that unrelenting way of hers. But Mrs. Scott didn't scare me so much anymore. I'd seen for myself what Malachi had said, just because someone had a temper, didn't mean they weren't kind. Besides, when Mrs. Scott got mad it was usually because she'd gotten protective of someone or some horse. "Honest, Mrs. Scott." I returned her stare, unblinking. "There was nothing bullying about it. I . . . I thought it was at first, but I was mistaken."

Mrs. Scott waited in that steely silence she always used to illicit truth. She must have learned that from her daddy, the prosecutor. It was intimidating as heck. It always made me squirm inside and wonder if maybe I actually had done something wrong that I wasn't remembering correctly. But I held my ground on this one. I was certain about that chestnut. "Truly," I said. "He was just showing off to get her to join him."

After a moment, she pursed her lips and said quietly, "Well, we certainly won't be working for that height. We're simply aiming for you two to have a lovely clean round of three-foot fences at the show. That's challenge enough." Letting go of my foot, she stepped back. "That's enough for him today."

Dismounting, I loosened his girth, tucked the stirrups up so they wouldn't bang against his scars, and started for the gate. Mrs. Scott followed me. "We're going to try something else now. I'm going to ride Cloud as you work out Caspian."

I turned to her in surprise. I'd only seen her ride that one time, when she was helping me search for Vivian when my little sister had run away so upset.

"What?" Mrs. Scott's eyebrow shot up. "Have Ralph or Malachi been filling your head with stories about me?"

Another test. "No, ma'am. Not stories. Just . . . just that you no longer rode." I wanted to add that I thought her not riding was a real shame, given how much she clearly loved horses, no matter her bluster. But fear about how she might react to my making such an observation kept me quiet.

"Did they say why?"

"N-n-no, ma'am." I wasn't about to get Malachi

in trouble by admitting he'd shared that it had something to do with whatever terrible thing had happened to her daughter because of the chestnut.

Mrs. Scott's gaze bore a hole through me. She knew I was fibbing. But—for the very first time—she let it go. "Necessity makes unexpected demands. Given the added debt from my deal with Mr. Berryman, I need to sell Cloud, too. Can't be helped. If I'm very fortunate, Evelyn will fall in love with both Cloud and Caspian. She does seem to have a soft spot for dappled-grays. She can afford to pay top dollar—I won't mind pressing her for a high price. A very high price."

Tugging at the knot of her ever-present throat scarf, Mrs. Scott went on, "So, in addition to entering you in the show on the chestnut, I will ride Cloud. Show judges love horses that are nimble and willing like those two are, horses that naturally position themselves well to a fence. We should ribbon on both of them. More important to our purposes, foxhunters who attend the show are watching for horses that stay calm, collected, and agreeable, who safeguard their riders. What could be a better display of Caspian's and Cloud's gentle dispositions and suitability for the fox hunt than their performing without the slightest fuss for a green teenager and"—Mrs. Scott gave me one of her rare smiles as she added—"a gray-haired woman."

She started toward the barn. "Besides, it's not fair for all the pressure to be on you, Beatrice."

When we entered the stable, Mrs. Scott stopped at Charity. She rubbed the mare's forehead and whispered, "Don't worry, you old beauty. You're not going anywhere unless they take me out first." Then she moved to Cloud. "What do you think, fella? Like old times?" She kissed his muzzle.

I stared. Mrs. Scott could be sweet? Sentimental? Was hell freezing over, too?

Perhaps sensing my amazement, she switched to her characteristic abruptness. "I need to be up on Evelyn's mare to train her anyway." She shrugged, rubbing Cloud's ears, still talking more to him than to me. "I have no idea if Evelyn's mare can be trained to jump. No one has taken her to a fence yet. That bet with Evelyn was more about building a relationship with an excellent rider who has lots of cash and a big stable that she wants to fill with good horses—like Caspian and Cloud. My winning our wager about the mare is a total long shot."

She sighed, thoughtful. "I won't know my chances with that mare until I know more of her personality. No trainer, no matter how good she might be—" Mrs. Scott paused and drifted into a sad voice, like the one I'd overheard her using when talking to Malachi that night in her study. "No trainer can put jump into a horse, can she, old boy? It's either there or it isn't—that inborn bounce and courage. A *good* trainer merely hones and schools what is innate. I learned that the hard way. To understand that I have to heed what a horse . . . or a person . . . has the heart and desire for. Sometimes, it's just not in them . . . no matter how hard I try to make it be." She nodded to herself and whispered, "That was my mistake."

I had no idea what to say. I stayed frozen in silence, like you do when a beautiful bird lands on your windowsill and you don't want to scare it off.

Was she talking about a horse? Or . . . or was she talking about her daughter?

If Mrs. Scott was talking about her daughter, her constantly testing me, pushing me—assessing my skills, my resolve, my heart and desire—made more sense. It wasn't *just* about her being all uppity and bossy and opinionated.

I felt awash in . . . in . . . I couldn't name it. I wished Vivian was with us because she'd just blurt out whatever this was tugging at my heart. I wanted to tell Mrs. Scott not to worry about me—that I wanted to jump every and any fence she put in front of me—with all my heart. And that the chestnut wanted to take me—I could feel it in him.

But before I could find the right words we were interrupted.

HONK-HONK. HONK-HONK-HONNNKK.

"What in the blue blazes," Mrs. Scott muttered, straightening back up to her usual ramrod posture. "I wasn't expecting Evelyn's mare to arrive until this afternoon. And why is that fool driver making such a racket?" She walked out into the driveway.

But it wasn't a horse trailer—it was a truck painted like a carnival caravan and a man that—well, a man so outrageous and loud in his appearance that even Mrs. Scott gaped at him. He flung open his door to stand on his seat, one booted foot braced on the open door's rolled-down window. His orange-red hair stood straight up from his head like a chrysanthemum. His shirt was blousy crimson gingham and on his wrists were multiple watches.

Pointing at Mrs. Scott and brandishing a long metal spear ending in a crown of stars, he shouted, "Hellllllllllooooooo, little lady! Behold your deliverance." He thumped his chest. "It is I, Dr. J. O. S. Chatman—rainmaker!"

CHAPTER 25

"Oh, for pity's sake," Mrs. Scott spluttered. "Shoo. Get off my property, you charlatan."

But Dr. Chatman simply dropped from his truck to the ground, clutching his chest, pretending she'd shot a shaft to his heart. "Charlatan? Why, ma'am, you cut me to the quick. But perhaps—" He grinned, so wide I could see gold caps on a few of his teeth. "Perhaps you meant to say Charlamagne. Because like Charlamagne the Great, I conquer all I see, defeating drought, and making it"—he shot his hands heavenward and bellowed—"RAIN! Rain, glorious, soaking, life-saving RAIN!"

My mouth dropped open.

Mrs. Scott took a few steps forward and crossed her arms in front of her. "No, I meant exactly what I said. Humbug. Fake. Swindler. I've read about you in the newspaper—bamboozling farmers to pay you fifteen cents an acre on the promise you'd bring them rain for their dying crops. You're a jackal, preying on despair. Go away. Leave the good people of this county alone."

"Why, little lady—"

"I am no little lady, you flimflammer."

He grinned, flashing gold. "Well now, beautiful, can't a man compliment—"

With a dismissive wave of her hand, Mrs. Scott stopped him cold again. "I no longer fall for shameless or ridiculous flattery, sir. I've met many a man like you. I mean it—get back in your truck."

"Ma'am, you might want to hear who sent me before you shoo me off so unceremoniously. I was invited here, you see. Sent for specifically."

Mrs. Scott harrumphed. "Indeed? By whom?"

"By some of my New York friends. Your new neighbors. Horsemen who are familiar with my good work—such as keeping rain off the Westchester Pacing Association's racetrack before an important high-stakes meet. There was a heavy rain that day in the metropolis, but that track, why, ma'am, that track remained dry as a bone and safe for the race thanks to me, Dr. J. O. S. Chatman, and the science of pluviculture. Those gents were so grateful, they paid me eight thousand dollars—hard cash testament to my abilities and successes."

"Eight thousand dollars? Good Lord, they are bigger fools than I thought, then."

Dr. Chatman ignored her. "Now, how did I achieve such a miracle, you might ask—"

"I didn't."

But Dr. Chatman kept talking, brandishing his weather-vane spear. "Why, ma'am, I'll tell you. By my expert knowledge of thermurgy, pneumaturgy, meteorolurgy—"

"Those are nonsense words," Mrs. Scott tried to interrupt.

"—by firing barrages to concuss the very clouds of heaven. Impellant, propellant, and disruptive charges on the proper angles according to the declination and inclination of the meridians, datum elevation, topography and geological strata, and astrophysical coordinates—"

"Stop!" Mrs. Scott held up her hands.

This time Dr. Chatman finally did—out of wind from all those big words, more than obeying her.

Just as he took in a deep breath to begin again, Rex came running, pushing the emptied wheelbarrow in front of him. "Hot dog!" He let go of the handles and wiped off his hands before enthusiastically shaking that of Dr. Chatman. "Grandpop told me you was a'coming."

Rex turned to Mrs. Scott. "This is the best dang news of the summer! Grandpop said to tell you, Mrs. Scott, with all due respect—and I hope you remember that I'm just doing the repeating he told me—that nothing ventured, nothing gained. And that you should try to use your imagination, if this here rainmaker came to your house." Rex nodded his head enthusiastically before tiptoeing to the truck's flatbed to eyeball its jammed-in contents: big bass drums, tall metal poles, bales of wire, and things that looked like Flash Gordon spaceships.

"Using my imagination with this snake-oil salesman is not the problem," Mrs. Scott replied. "And tell your Grandpop that he will be hearing from me on this subject."

"Say, I could use an assistant," crowed the rainmaker. "What's your name, boy?"

Rex beamed. "Rex Welty Williams. Rex means—"

"King!" Dr. Chatman bellowed. "Hail, fellow! And well met. You're my kind of soul. A king has vision, dreams for his people, the fortitude to discount and dispel the doubts of the fearful. How would you like to help me bring"—he threw his arms heavenward again—"RAIN!"

"You serious, mister? Geez, that'd be swell."

"Oh no." Mrs. Scott had finally had it. She walked over to the truck herself. "No, no, no. I need you here, Rex." She put her hand on his shoulder as his face fell in disappointment. "Please go help Beatrice tack up Cloud and Caspian." Rex did seem to perk up a bit at my name, which somehow made me want to run for the hills.

"Now, you," she turned to Dr. Chatman. "I want you to get back in your truck and drive away."

The rainmaker made an elaborate bow. "I don't stay where I'm not wanted or not understood. Your wish is my command, ma'am." He stayed bent over and added, "But . . . perhaps I should share that I was sent by a man at the bank and some of his fox-chasing brethren." Dr. Chatman straightened up. His voice had changed from theatrical and courtly to cool and a little threatening, if you ask me. "You see, ma'am," he continued, "the hunt is worried that this drought will continue through next month. And if it does, the ground will be too dry for the hounds to take the scent when fox-hunting season opens."

"Ah, I see. And I was thinking it was out of concern for the farmers."

"Well now, ma'am, I suppose they are plenty worried about the hay fields. After all, what would they give their horses to eat if those fail?" Dr. Chatman gazed over her head toward Mrs. Scott's knee-high alfalfa meadows. "I suspect you're counting on your hay crop as well. Shame about everyone's corn."

Pursing her lips, Mrs. Scott chewed on that for a moment. "What is it you want—exactly?"

He smiled, seeing he'd landed a small hit on her. "These influential . . . and rather important gentlemen I mentioned—I'm sure you know them well and that they believe in making things happen when they've come to a decision—these *respected* gentlemen have asked me to construct a series of apparatuses. Towers. Like radio aerials, with wires strung down to low-lying earth and grounded with iron bars and plates of copper and zinc. Those aerials create electrical attraction that seduces clouds to gather, one," he gestured to the sky, "after another," he spun round looking heavenward, "after another."

He took a few steps toward Mrs. Scott. "Once there are enough clouds bumping up against one another, I shoot up charges of dynamite. Straight into the bellies of all that cumulous and nimbostratus. Rattling their fluffy innards and hastening precipitation."

Planting his feet wide, Dr. Chatman looked about to crow like some silly proud rooster. "It works best when the aerials are on high ground. I've installed several on the adjacent fields, with one of your neighbors, courtesy of the hunt gentlemen. I—and they—would like to put a few here on your lovely rolling hills as well, ma'am. Spread that electrical magnetism as far as possible." He looked upward, sweeping his arm along the horizon until he paused, holding his hand aloft. "Why, look there!" He pointed to the tiniest brushstroke of white in the hot blue sky. "Cirrus clouds! It is already working!"

Mrs. Scott did not look upward.

Slowly, Dr. Chatman lowered his arm.

"These towers of yours sound like nothing

other than large lightning rods," she began. "Or firetraps. And firing off dynamite will only scare the local dairy cows silly and dry up their milk. Or send my horses into a panicked stampede that's sure to bring serious injury to one of them. If I catch you near my property doing any of your hogwash, I will run you off myself. Now," Mrs. Scott gestured to the truck, "good day, sir."

Dr. Chatman opened his mouth to let fly some other barnstormer speech, but Mrs. Scott simply repeated, "Good day, sir."

This time, the rainmaker seemed to relent. But as he climbed back onto his truck's running board, he needled her, "My backers, my friends from New York, will be mighty disappointed. Migh-ty dis-a-ppoin-ted. You know the thing about doubt, ma'am? It deflates . . . it dissipates . . . it deadens. The heavens don't respond to lack of faith. As a God-fearing woman—I'm assuming you are a churchgoing lady—and as such you know that. Why," he scanned the sky, "I'd hate to be the one who ruins it for everyone else." He lowered his gaze to hers and smiled coolly, no gold showing this time.

Mrs. Scott frowned. "Get . . . off . . . my . . . land."

"Suit yourself." He swung himself into the truck. "I tried. Don't blame me if you lose everything. Or . . . your neighbors do." The rainmaker waved out the window at me. "So long, little lady!"

Watching to make sure he truly exited, Mrs. Scott didn't budge until the truck left her long drive. Then, in the distance, we could hear a faint *honk-honk-honk*, as Dr. J. O. S. Chatman descended upon another neighbor.

"The fools," she grumbled. "I suppose they are so rich and so used to getting their way that they think they can buy anything—including rain."

Shaking her head, Mrs. Scott started back to the stable, muttering. "I certainly know how to make enemies . . . and annoy the few friends I have left."

She kicked a stone at her foot and looked back

to me. "Well, I just made our job at the horse show a lot harder. There'll probably be a group of jackasses rooting against me now because of my turning away that ridiculous so-called rain-maker . . . on top of those who were disgruntled about the Berryman auction." She sighed, her walk slowing. "And gossiping . . . as if that were anything new." She stopped dead. "Oh God. Now I have to be extra charming at that party Evelyn invited me to this weekend."

Mrs. Scott made herself walk on. "I hate having to be charming."

CHAPTER 26

Several days later, Vivian gasped and clapped her hands when she saw Mrs. Scott dressed for the theater lady's party. "Ooh, you look like a fairy queen!"

We were sitting on the porch, reading *Treasure Island* together, one of the books from her sons' collection that they obviously loved dearly, its spine and pages frayed from turning. I reached out to stop her as she jumped off the swing, but Vivian darted away to dance around her, chirping, "Golly,

Mrs. Scott. You look all different. So pretty."

"Viv!" I needed to teach her how to say things politely. Although I was a bit stunned myself by Mrs. Scott's appearance.

She wore a chemise dress of pale-blue chiffon, decorated all over with clusters of crystal beads in little reflective starbursts. Its drop-hip waist was laced through horizontally with silver metal thread. She'd wrapped a long strand of pearls around her neck several times, which then almost fell to her waist. Long glittery earrings dangled below her bobbed gray hair. She even wore glamour lipstick and mascara that made those already searing-scary violet eyes of hers look darker and even more all-knowing.

"What?" Vivian asked me as she gazed up admiringly at Mrs. Scott. "Look at her. She's all shimmery and lovely."

I don't know why I still expected her to be unkind to Vivian, but I reflexively held my breath until Mrs. Scott spoke. "That's very kind of you, child, since this dress is at least ten years old. Completely out of style. But then again, so am I. And it's what I had in my closet."

Groaning, Mrs. Scott pulled on long white gloves. "These will be murder in this heat. Why in the world would one have a dinner party requiring formal attire when it's a hundred degrees in the shade? Utter nonsense." She tugged at the pearls to loosen them a bit from her throat.

"Beatrice," she began.

"Yes, ma'am?"

"As I dressed, I was thinking about that chestnut. Thinking about what I would say this evening about him, to set the stage for us at the horse show. And about you." She considered me a moment. "We should change his name. I always think of him simply as 'the chestnut' or, when I am angry, 'the Black Tuesday horse' because he has been so . . . calamitous. But that certainly won't work—reminding people of the stock market crash. Bad luck and superstition and all. And the name his previous owner gave him—Vulcan—is rather unfortunate as well. I suppose the man chose it out of some misguided machismo—for all his ill-temper, Vulcan was the husband of Venus."

She paused. "We can allude to the chestnut's coloring, but it should be positive. And I think the new name should reflect the change in him. Any ideas?"

"You're . . . you're asking me?"

"Unless there is someone else here named Beatrice." Her voice softened a bit as she added, "Did you know the name Beatrice means 'voyager' or 'one who brings gladness'?"

I didn't. For just a moment, I felt the way I had when Mama had caught me up for a quick "just because" hug.

Mrs. Scott kept talking. "You're the one who has wrought this turnaround. You should do the honors. You know him the best. Think of his attributes."

Dozens of words raced through my mind: Jaunty. Flying. Freedom. Power. Then my heart spoke up: Joy. Friendship. Love. I swallowed against a lump that suddenly filled my throat. I remembered the sense of wonderment I felt as the sun rose warm and crimson while I sat on him, frozen in time, bareback. The moment I could feel the chestnut shed his fear and begin to trust me.

Daybreak. First light. A new day.

Which could mean a new chance. A new deal even—for him, for me—just like Dr. Liburn had said that FDR man was promising a country on its knees.

Hope.

"Sunup," I blurted out. "Sunup, the New Deal Horse."

"Oh, I like that, Bea!" Vivian clapped again.

Mrs. Scott nodded, thinking. "I like it as well. Done. That will be his full show name. We'll call him Sunup for short." She patted Vivian's head and smiled at me—a lovely, breaking-day kind of smile. "Don't stay up too late. I expect to find you abed when I return. We'll be riding early in the morning per usual. Only two weeks now till the show. We'll begin with the—with your Sunup."

With that, Mrs. Scott departed—driving herself to a fancy party in a glittery Roaring Twenties dress and a back-firing pickup truck—leaving me dumbfounded. Sunup. *My* Sunup. A new deal.

Before that instant, I hadn't really let myself

think about the cost of Mrs. Scott's plan if it worked. My focus had just been on proving my worth to her in the orchard and fields, then around her stable. Of giving her a reason to let my little sister and me stay. Then it was to show how well I could ride, and that the chestnut was worth saving. I hadn't really, cross-my-heart-honest faced the cold-hard fact that if I rode the chestnut—Sunup, *my* Sunup—well enough at the show, if we sailed over the fences, clean and scopey and gorgeous, she would sell him. To save her home. To feed us. He'd be gone.

My heart broke.

If I had learned one thing, it was to try to savor every fleeting moment of happiness for all it was worth, as spiritual vitamins against the soul-sickening hard times. I hadn't known to do that while Mama was alive to ward against the ache of her being gone. Or about home, to steel myself to survive the terrible day-to-day unknowns of not having one with the faith that things once had been and so therefore could be better. No one had warned me that life could turn on a dime and with the force of an earthquake.

But I sure knew it now.

I had fourteen days. I was going to ride Sunup as many times as I possibly could in that fortnight's precious daylight hours, for every single solitary minute I could. To memorize the feel of that bliss. I went to the stable to jump Sunup before twilight dropped. Ignoring the one rule Mrs. Scott had given me about him—to never ride him alone.

Rex had already turned the horses out to graze and romp. Sound carried so far along those open pastures, I could hear the retreating sound of his singing. *Forget your troubles, c'mon get happy. You better chase all your cares away . . .*

Precisely what I hoped to do.

Reaching the pasture fence, I started to whistle and call to him. But the chestnut—Sunup—spotted me from across the field and came cantering, tail high, nickering his hello. He was gathering such momentum, I thought he might jump the fence to reach me.

"Whoa, boy, whoa." I held up my hands to slow him and darned if he didn't listen. I swear the way he tossed his head as he stopped, he was thinking, *aww, come on.*

I grinned. "Hey, boy." I stroked his beautiful coppery neck, and he tucked his muzzle into my shoulder, holding it there quietly, breathing hot, grassy breath into my face. "Guess what, fella? You have a new name: Sunup, the New Deal Horse. Whatta you think?" He nibbled my shirt and held the fabric in his teeth, tugging on it playfully. I laughed. "Let's go for a ride, okay?"

Following me down the fence line to the stable, Sunup stood absolutely still as I tacked him up and when I climbed the mounting block. I swung myself onto his back, and he walked on with a buoyant prance. Closing my eyes, I memorized the feel of that merry *clip-clop-clip-clop.*

"Traw-aw-ot."

Like Vivian skipped with delight, Sunup hop-kicked up into a floaty trot. I posted, raising myself off his saddle in rhythm with his stride—now just a tad of a lift like Mrs. Scott had taught me, my legs properly glued to his side, after all those aching hours of riding without stirrups. I memorized the sensation of being in perfect harmony with another living being, this astoundingly graceful and powerful creature. For the first time I could feel the way Mrs. Scott looked on Cloud—simply an extension of a magnificent horse.

Sliding my outside leg back slightly, I pressed my inside calf to his ribs to signal Sunup to canter. He transitioned, smooth as silk. *Da-da-dum, da-da-dum, da-da-dum.*

We waltzed around and around, his cadence unwavering, steady, fluid—graceful and stunningly athletic at the same time. Just the way he needed to approach a high fence. I turned him to the course of three-foot-high jumps Mrs. Scott had set up earlier in the day. He nickered with happy anticipation as we started toward the first fence and its stack of red-and-white-striped poles.

Ten strides away . . . Eight . . . Four . . . Two.

That's when the sky exploded.

Sssssssss . . . . Ssssssssss . . . Pop-pop-pop—BANG! Pop-pop-pop—BANG!

With a shrieking, panicked whinny, Sunup reared.

I managed to grab hold his mane. Oh God, we were right on top of the jump. "Sunup," I cried. "Whoa! Whoa!"

Ssssssss . . . Pop-pop-pop—BANG!

Sunup thrashed his front legs as he stood—as if fighting off another horse attacking him. I lurched around on his back, clinging to his mane. "Whoa! Please! Whoa!"

Sssssss . . . Pop-pop-pop—BANG!

Then, as frantic as if a wrathful storm had blown up, Sunup dropped down to bolt for cover. His front shoulder dipped. He twisted to the side. He surged away. All in a flash of frenetic contortion.

I went flying off him. Hit wood—wood—wood. The ground. Blinding pain.

Ssssss . . . Pop-pop-pop—BANG!

I felt myself yanked by my foot. Violently jerked.

My foot. My foot was caught in the stirrup! *Whoa! Whoa!*

I was being dragged. Felt sand raking my arms. Choking on dirt. *Stop! Please!*

Then I felt nothing.

CHAPTER 27

"Bea! Bea!"

"Easy, Viv, easy. Don't spook the horse. Help me now. Show me where your sister's caught."

I felt hands—one small, two large and strong—on my foot, lifting it away from an iron vise. Knifing pain. I wanted to cry out but couldn't. I was too deep down in darkness. Had twilight already come?

Hot breath on my face.

"Push that horse back away from your sister. Careful now, child. Hold onto his reins. If he gives you any trouble, let go."

"But he'll step on her if I do."

"If he aimed to hurt her, he would have already."

I felt my leg propped up on a knee. My boot being unlaced—each buttonhole unstrung felt like being beaten with a crop. Sock slowly rolled down to my toes. Were those my toes? That's where they should be. But all I felt was horrible throbbing-throbbing-throbbing.

"Not broken. Thank you, Lord."

Cool linen on my ankle. Wrapping. Quick, around my heel, my arch, and up. Tight. Tighter still. Tight. The throbbing eased.

"Where did you learn that?"

"In a very dark forest in France, called the Argonne."

Could someone stop the swarm of bees in my head, please?

"Listen to me carefully, Viv. Take that horse to his stall and lock him in. You need to get Rex to help carry her to the house. Ralph doesn't have a phone. It's a long way, child. Almost a mile. Think you can make it?"

"Yes, sir, Mr. Malachi."

"Go past my cottage, then through the cornfields—keeping straight where they are widest. Pick your way across the creek and then up a hill and over. You'll see his house."

I heard *clip-clop-clip* away.

I felt my mouth move. Viv? Viv? She needed to take his saddle off or Sunup might be afraid. Viv?

"Shh, now, Beatrice. You're all right. I just need help getting you inside. Lie quiet until Rex gets here."

I heard humming. Soft and baritone. I felt a man's hand on my forehead, gentle. Daddy? Oh, is that you, Daddy? Have you come home?

"Shh, honeylamb. Rest."

Then once again, nothing.

WHOA! PLEASE. WHOA!

I came to shouting, and Viv hurled herself at me, nearly choking me in her embrace. "I thought you were dead!" She pulled back, her eyes enormous. "You scared me!" She punched my shoulder.

"Don't ever do that again!"

"Ouch!" I tried to push her away, but the ache in my arms stopped me short.

"Goodness, child. She's bruised enough!" Mrs. Scott pulled Vivian away from me. "Although I feel the same sentiments." The two of them stood beside the bed, glowering at me.

My head was swimming. "What . . . what happened?"

"You did precisely what I told you not—" Mrs. Scott began.

"I saved you!" Vivian exclaimed, cutting her off, and bouncing up and down on her toes. "Well . . . me and Mr. Malachi did."

"Mr. Malachi and I," Mrs. Scott corrected.

Vivian rolled her eyes. I reflexively winced, thinking about how much my head would hurt if I tried the same. "The world was exploding—," she began.

"Curse that rainmaker," Mrs. Scott muttered.

"—with all sorts of whizzings and bangs. I didn't know what was happening! So I ran to find you. And there you were on the ground. The chestnut—I mean Sunup—was standing beside you, shaking all over. There was a jump that was all smashed. Your foot was hanging in the stirrup. You wouldn't answer me. I didn't know what to do! The sky was still exploding. I thought maybe the world was ending or a war was starting or . . . or . . . I don't know what. Thank goodness for Mr. Malachi, because he was already trying to find his way down the hill to me. I might have been screaming." Her face puckered, embarrassed. "I don't rightly know. But when I explained how you were lying on the ground like a ragdoll, he told me to show him, fast."

Viv pointed to my foot. "He tore off his sleeve and wrapped your ankle, quick as a wink. Dr. Liburn says it's a sprain, but it would have been a lot worse if Mr. Malachi hadn't wrapped it so well and so fast and that it was a tragedy, a . . . well, I shouldn't say the word Dr. Liburn used . . . but a terrible something about the fact Mr. Malachi hadn't been able to go to medical school the way he had hoped because of his eyes being ruined by being beaten for parading. I didn't know that about Mr. Malachi, did you, Bea? That he—"

I thought my head would explode if my little sister didn't pipe down.

Mrs. Scott must have sensed that Viv's chatter was making a thunderstorm in my head because she put her hand on Viv's shoulder to quiet her. "You are lucky, Beatrice," she said to me in a low voice. "It could have been worse." She caught her breath with a tiny shudder, like she'd been poked in her side. "Much worse."

"Sunup, is he all right?" I asked.

"He's fine. Although he's lucky I didn't strangle him when I first heard you were hurt."

"You should have seen her," Vivian blurted, "she was furious and acting all unhinged. Dr. Liburn says she was in shock, but I've never seen—"

"Vivian, child, come with me." Malachi had been sitting by the window the whole time. He took her hand and tugged Viv toward the door. "Mrs. Scott needs to talk to your sister." I could hear him explaining as they walked down the hallway, "In the army they call it shell shock. Some soldiers—when they come home, they seem fine until suddenly something reminds them of the terrible things they saw in battle. They relive it and . . ." his voice faded away and I couldn't hear the rest.

Mrs. Scott pulled up a chair. "So," she said as she sat and leaned forward. "Did the chestnut pull a dirty stop on you? Because if he did—"

Vehemently, I shook my head, and then had to put my hands to my forehead to stop the clanging inside. "No, ma'am. He spooked. There was a terrible explosion of some sort just as he was about to take the fence. It scared him and he reared. Last thing I remember is flying off and hitting the poles and the ground . . . and . . ." I trailed off.

"Being dragged?"

Would she hold that against him? Would I?

Her eyebrows shot up.

"Maybe?"

She nodded. "I went down to the ring. I saw the drag mark. A remarkable thing had happened."

I held my breath.

"He stopped. He could have dragged you across the entire arena. But he didn't. He stopped within four or five strides, it looks like. And Malachi claims he kept vigil over you until Vivian moved him away." Mrs. Scott pursed her lips and sat back. "As long as he didn't dirty dump you."

"Is . . . is that what happened with your daughter?" I whispered.

Mrs. Scott looked to the floor, looked out the window, and then back to me. "I'm not sure it's really your business, young lady."

I was feeling fear bubbling up in me about Sunup. I needed to know what had happened before with him. I held my ground. "If I am going to ride him, I need to know."

Scowling, Mrs. Scott got up and paced. After a few moments she said, "That is reasonable." With a heavy sigh, she sat down again. "Yes. A dirty, dirty stop. At a stone wall I told her to take. We were out on a hack with a large number of hunters. No ballyhooing hounds, no fox. Just going cross-country to get the chestnut acclimated again."

Closing her eyes, she rubbed her forehead, hard—like she wanted to wipe clean a horrible memory—before opening them again and continuing. "The chestnut approached at a good pace. Looked like he was gathering himself to leap. But then . . . he . . . he stopped dead at the base of the wall, sharp, at the very last minute, and ducked away, hurling her forward. My daughter slammed into the rocks. Hard. It . . . the force of the way he threw her, it shattered her leg.

"I rode forward to grab his reins, shouting at her to get her foot loose from the stirrup. I was terrified that he might . . ."

"Drag her," I whispered.

Mrs. Scott nodded. "The scream that came out of her as she did . . ." Mrs. Scott sucked in a breath and shuddered. "Was terrible. Wrenching her foot free worsened the break, causing a spiral fracture up the calf bone. She was delirious with pain . . ." Mrs. Scott held her hand to her mouth for a few moments as if she might throw up. "And anger. Said I cared more about stopping the horse from running away than if she were hurt. Which was untrue. I was trying to hold the chestnut still so she wouldn't get hurt even worse. But . . . the other things she shouted . . . were completely justified.

She hasn't spoken to me since."

"But . . . but why is she mad at you?"

"She is not like you, Beatrice. Not like your mama. Not like me. And not like my sons. I see that now. But I wanted her to be. And I pushed her. Tried to put the jump in her, as it were. I could see her hesitation. But I foolishly decided the best way to dispel that was for her to prove to herself that she could handle riding a fancy horse like that chestnut. To help me train him and then compete at the highest levels. I was wrong. And it cost Marjorie. There was surgery and weeks in a wheelchair. And now a very stiff, weak leg. She limps. She's lost her ability to dance the way she and her husband used to, the way I now know she had always loved."

Mrs. Scott fidgeted. "After my sons died, I . . . I missed them so dreadfully. I think I poured all their dreams onto her. It wasn't fair. I failed to see and support who *she* was. Marjorie rode tentatively. And that chestnut—your Sunup—sensed it. A horse will refuse if he doesn't trust his rider to take him to a fence in a way he can safely clear it. Both the horse and rider have to believe in one another."

Mrs. Scott looked at me, her dark eyes piercing. "Like he and you do." She let that sink in for a few beats.

Then she held up that pointer finger of hers. "It's not like there isn't always the chance of something going wrong, dreadfully wrong, in riding. But . . ." She crossed her arms. "Your fall today? From what you tell me, it would not have happened had it not been for that idiot rainmaker shooting explosives into the air. And seeing how Sunup stopped in his tracks and kept watch over you while you were on the ground—even as frightened as he was—tells me that you two will probably be able to do just about anything together."

She nodded. Then stood. "Dr. Liburn says that Malachi's wrapping kept your ankle from swelling badly. He thinks if you rest for a few days with the foot elevated, you might be able to still ride in the show. That is," she paused, "only if you wish to."

Did I? I closed my eyes against the feel of hitting

fencepoles. Concentrated to replace it with the joyous sensation of sailing over a jump. Oh yes. I propped myself up on my elbows to answer, "Yes, ma'am. I want to."

"You are certain? Don't say yes out of sheer stubbornness, or because you don't want to admit being uncertain. Or because of our plans." Eyeing me closely, Mrs. Scott waited.

Stubbornness? Was that all bad? If it meant staying strong in the face of terrible things and not giving up, it seemed a pretty good trait to me. One that had kept me kicking and swimming against tides that were doing their darnedest to drag me and Viv under. And one that obviously had kept Mrs. Scott resilient and tenacious during her hard times. This woman had been kind to my sister and me. Taken us in out of the blue. Stood by us even when we made trouble for her. It was my turn to help her by making it to the show.

I nodded slightly, just like she always did when she decided a thing. "Can't take the jump out of me, Mrs. Scott."

Mrs. Scott smiled—one of those lovely real ones. “All right, then. And now,” she moved to the door, “I have a few choice words to say to that rainmaker.”

Dr. J. O. S. Chatman left the county the next day.

CHAPTER 28

The Warrenton Horse Show had a grandstand. A big one. Full of people. In garden party dresses and linen suits, fanning themselves with folded programs. Lots and lots and lots of people. Applauding riders for clear rounds. Gasping at clumsy approaches to fences. Groaning when a horse knocked down a rail. Watching every flick of a horse's tail, every twitch in the saddle by a rider that took place in the mowed grass arena, still velvety green despite the drought.

Beyond that structure, more people stood on

the hill, some balancing on the hoods of their parked trucks to see. Somewhere up there was Vivian, holding Ralph's hand. He had come with Rex, announcing that Mrs. Scott never did braid a horse's mane properly for a show and only he could do it for us. Mrs. Scott had seemed awfully glad to see him, despite all her fussing that he had no business taxing his broken arm that way. And he answered her to leave off, he was fit as a fiddle.

Scanning what faces I could see at that distance, I hoped some of them were friendly. I'd never ridden in front of an audience before. Much less a huge one.

"Don't catch flies, young lady."

I snapped my mouth shut. Easy for Mrs. Scott to say. This hoopla was second nature to her. Tightening my grip on Caspian's reins with one hand, I tugged at the stock tie she'd threaded around my neck with the other. I couldn't breathe. Beads of sweat were oozing down my back under my jacket. Under my borrowed velveteen helmet, my hair was matted to my skull. And the wrap Malachi had wound tight around my ankle felt burning hot, as if I had a fur muff on. But it was doing its duty. My foot felt fine in the stirrup. Now if the rest of me would just hold together.

Unlike me, Caspian stood absolutely quiet, unruffled by the noise and the flags and the two dozen other thoroughbreds jigging in place, waiting to enter the ring, one by one.

I glanced down at Mrs. Scott. In that oppressive heat, she wore even fancier formal attire than I did—a short-waisted and buttoned jacket that had tails like men wore to black-tie balls, a jabot at her throat, and a top hat. And yet she still looked crisp. Pristine.

She'd caused quite a stir earlier, in fact, among competitors sitting in front of the show's stables and temporary tack rooms as we passed on the way to the warm-up ring.

"Mrs. Scott!" I recognized the man who had come out of the bank, counting cash he'd just withdrawn, on the first day she'd taken me into the village. "You are riding?" He was standing in front of his stall encampment. He'd actually hung up a chandelier above his racks of saddles and covered the walls with brocade fabric and paintings of foxhunting and English setters carrying dead quails in their mouths. Blue ribbons from past horseshow wins hung over the stall doors of the six horses he'd brought to compete.

"I certainly am, Mr. Carlson," Mrs. Scott had replied. "I am sure you wish me the very best of luck."

Gesturing toward his horses, all of them gorgeous, sleek, and muscular, groomed so they gleamed, the man countered, "You will need it, I am afraid." He was trying to fake good-natured ribbing, but it still came out sounding like a snarl from a dog protecting a bone. Then he said, all make-believe concern, "I hear there was a bit of trouble at your place."

"Yes, there was." Mrs. Scott answered flatly.

His expression turned icy—no more play-acting. "Shame about the rainmaker."

"Yes, it was." It was clear Mrs. Scott didn't mean the comment the way Mr. Carlson put it.

"Is your daughter riding with you today?" He was smirking.

I wanted to kick him. But Mrs. Scott laughed lightly. "Goodness no. She doesn't have time to come down from Philadelphia for this."

Overhearing this exchange, another competitor approached. He wore foxhunting "pinks" and a bowler hat. I couldn't tell for sure, because it had happened so quickly the day of the auction, but I could have sworn it was the man who'd grinned in respect at Mrs. Scott before driving off in his maroon Packard. "Good day, Millicent. It's good to see you competing again," he said. "Although given your attire, I fear we might be entered against one another."

Mrs. Scott smiled sincerely at this man. "Yes, we seem to be meeting once more in the stakes class."

When the man grinned, I recognized him for sure. It was big and toothy and real. "I am counting on the outcome being different this year."

"Well, I certainly hope it is not."

He chortled before looking toward me. Seeming to read my presence exactly the way Mrs. Scott had hoped, he asked, "I'm looking to purchase a safe hunter for my daughter-in-law. It needs to be a packer. She knows next to nothing about the hunt, but she's game. A plucky girl. Any of your horses available? My wife loved that mare we procured from you. What, five years ago now, I think."

"Oh? Well, Paul, it would depend." Mrs. Scott smiled sweetly. "I am very fond of the two grays that Beatrice and I are riding today. They are so agreeable. True gentlemen schoolmasters. So I'd hate to part with them. But for a friend like you? And for a good price? I would certainly consider it." She pretended to think for a beat. "Caspian is going particularly nicely for Beatrice." She shrugged daintily. "Why don't you watch our rounds, and we can talk later?"

She bowed her head slightly. He tipped his bowler. We walked on to the warm-up ring. "One more fish on the line," she murmured.

Now I just needed to prove Mrs. Scott's claims about me.

As we watched the three riders ahead of me—Caspian's ears pricked up with interest, me nervously squirming in the saddle—I tried to memorize what the others were doing. The course had eight jumps, the sequence snaking and threading through them. A wrong turn or a fence out of order would disqualify me automatically.

Mrs. Scott talked me through their quirks. "See that sharp turn between the third and fourth jumps? Slow him so you can make the turn deep, to give yourself several straight-on strides before the takeoff. That single rail? That one that looks easy because it's less solid? That's actually the hardest jump out there because there is no ground reference to help Caspian judge its depth. You must do that for him. If you clear that fence, you'll be home free."

For the most part, the horses and riders were taking the course flawlessly. Mrs. Scott had had to enter me in a "working hunter" division on Caspian, with other experienced horses, because he'd jumped in shows before with her. Sunup and

I, on the other hand, would be in a "green hunter" class, where theoretically the competition should be less steep. That was the idea anyway.

The more I watched, the sicker I felt. I wanted to vomit. I was going to fail her. In this class, up against all these seasoned and accomplished riders, I was going to look like a total amateur. Caspian and I were going to come in last. Then no one would want to buy him. She was going to lose her farm.

One more rider to go.

Putting her hand on my knee, Mrs. Scott patted it. "Beatrice, take a deep breath now. You've done good work. Remember, it's not just clearing the fences. You will be judged on Caspian's way-of-going—is he safe and sure, moving at a uniform and smooth pace, in good control, with heart and honesty at the fence. You two have shown that day after day as we've schooled. Just do what you've done at home. Caspian knows his job out there. The judges—and ultimately the spectators—are going to be impressed by your youth. All the other riders are adults."

The announcer called my number.

Mrs. Scott nodded and stepped back from me as the previous rider trotted out of the gate. "Go have fun now."

Clucking my tongue at him, Caspian glided through the open gate and strutted past the grandstand. I swallowed back bile. He gave a gentle *watch-this-folks* toss of his head, ready, serenely confident.

The judge rang a little bell, telling me to start my round.

Leg on, leg on. Get contact with Caspian's mouth and the bit, get him collected. More leg. Leg. Squeeze, squeeze with each stride, get that momentum. *Da-da-dum. Da-da-dum.* Caspian waltzed in a circle, waiting for me to launch him toward the fences, patient, reassuring.

Okay. Here we go. *Da-da-dum. Da-da-dum. Da-da-dum.* First jump, double-crossed poles. Stride, stride, bounce, up—float—back to the ground, with a graceful, light touchdown. And away. *Da-da-dum. Da-da-dum.* On to the next. And the next.

Caspian was perfect. Perfect.

Until that single rail.

I tensed, choking up the reins. He hesitated. *Leg on. Leg on.* I corrected myself.

Caspian slid a little as we came to the rail. But he vaulted up, despite my mistake, sailed over, and—*click*.

I heard a mass groan.

His back hoof had clipped the rail, just barely, just a whisper, like the flick of a finger. No! No, no, no!

Rattle . . . rattle . . . the rail bobbled in its holding cups . . .

I rode on, dreading the *thunk* as the pole fell to the ground, announcing my failure. Sorry. So sorry.

Rattle . . . rattle . . .

Don't look back, don't look back, another fence is coming, I chided myself. Focus on Caspian. *Da-da-dum. Da-da-dum.*

Rattle . . . silence . . . I caught my breath as the rail stopped jiggling and settled into place—just as

Caspian lifted into the air and we sailed over the last fence.

The crowd erupted with applause.

But I only felt so much triumph as I brought Caspian down to a trot to exit the gate and then stand, with all the other riders and horses, waiting to be called back into the ring for the announcement of ribbons. Stupid, stupid mistake, I whipped myself. Well, the judges wouldn't rank anyone coming below eighth place. At least there was that, I thought. I would be spared the humiliation of being crowned dead last.

We came in fifth.

Wait—what? Fifth?

The judge had to shake the ribbon at me a little for me to believe, lean over, and take it. My very first ribbon. "Thank you," I murmured.

The judge touched the brim of his hat. "Solid ride," he said. "Great horse." He patted Caspian's neck and moved on to the rider pinned sixth.

"Well done!" Mrs. Scott beamed as we came out of the arena, a pink ribbon tucked into Caspian's bridle. She beamed—I swear.

"I'm so sorry I made that mistake. I—"

Mrs. Scott waved me off. "Honestly, that little hiccup of yours showed Caspian even more to perfection. He corrected for you, didn't he? Without any protest or fuss. His arc over that obstacle was still centered, not a hint of a run-out. The willing gentleman that he is. The judges liked that. And I promise Paul is going to be very interested in him for his daughter-in-law. If he bids against Evelyn, we will do very well."

"Yes, ma'am." I murmured, still a little rattled—just like that pole—by my mistake. Sunup was not Caspian. He would not be so tolerant.

Mrs. Scott assessed me before adding, "You corrected nicely as well, following his lead. Riding doesn't go like clockwork, Beatrice, it takes quick reads and reactions. The rest of your round was very polished. Lovely pacing. Wise. Steady." She patted my leg. "Ready for more?"

"Yes, ma'am." And I was.

But I still threw up in the bushes on the way back to our stall. My real test as a rider was yet to come, with Sunup. And if I was to be granted only one show ride with him before someone else bought him, I wanted it to be stupendous. A Milky Way of fireflies lighting up a nighttime forest kind of memory to hold up against dark days.

CHAPTER 29

Back at our show stalls, Vivian came darting. "BEA! You were a-mazing!" She skipped round and round as I got off Caspian. "A-mazing! A-mazing!"

Startled by her cavorting, Sunup started kicking his stall's walls.

"Child," Ralph grabbed hold of her. "Let's not cause a rumpus. I don't want to be Humpty Dumpty again. The doc might not be able to glue me back together another time."

Simmering down, Vivian lowered her voice to

an excited whisper, "A-mazing!" She took Ralph's hand. "Sorry, Mr. Ralph."

"Wish I'd aseen it," Rex grumbled. He'd stayed with the horses, brushing and saddling Cloud for Mrs. Scott, whose class was next. "Bet she was beautiful," he murmured to Caspian as he took him from me.

But I heard it. I thought I might have to head to the bushes again.

Ralph let out a long whistle. "That boy's got it bad."

Vivian looked up at his wrinkled face. "Got what?"

"He's been struck down by the lovey-dovey." He winked at me as Mrs. Scott swung herself up on Cloud and started toward the arena. "C'mon, Beatrice. You'll want to watch her round."

"I was going to groom Sunup."

"Rex will do that for you, young'un. And you need to stay focused," he tossed the last word loudly toward Rex. "Believe you me, you want to see Miss Milly ride." Tugging on Vivian, he followed behind Cloud singing another of his cheery songs, about flying in the face of cold hard Depression reality. Where Ralph got his optimism, all old and broken-up as he was, was a wonderment. *It's only a paper moon, sailing over a cardboard sea. But it wouldn't be make-believe if you believed in me . . .*

We came to a different arena from the one I had just ridden, where Mrs. Scott and about twenty other riders were milling around, waiting. They looked like they were headed to the opera or something, they were all so formal in their fancy coats and top hats. Mrs. Corker was in the ring, too, as well as that nasty Mr. Carlson and the man Mrs. Scott had called Paul who wanted a horse for his daughter-in-law. He trotted up to Mrs. Scott to chat. Mrs. Corker joined their conversation, and three abreast, they circled the arena.

"What class is this?" I asked.

"Working hunter stakes, over the outside course," Ralph explained. "The toughest competition of the day. And there's serious-as-a-skunk prize money. That's why she's entered it. Miss Milly wasn't much older than you when she won it for the first time. But she sure hasn't wanted to ride anything like this course since her daughter . . . Well, for a long spell. If she makes it through this," his voice hushed, "then she'll be all right again."

The horses and riders kept meandering.

"Are we waiting for the announcer?" I asked.

"Nope. They're all waiting to see who has the courage to go first—so they can watch and learn how hard the jumps are. To copycat a good ride or avoid that first rider's mistakes." He pointed out of the ring toward a wide, rolling pasture. "See those?"

I stood on tiptoe and craned my neck to see. High stone walls, pyramid-shaped solid wooden coops, snake post-and-rail fences—they all had to be four feet tall or more. There was also a mass of dead brush piled wide and high, topped with a thick log set on vertical rails. The thing had to be six feet wide and five feet tall. It looked like something you'd pile up outside a fort to stop an enemy army in its tracks. What in heavens' name was that?

Seeing where I was looking, gaping, Ralph

murmured, "The Aiken. That monster is what finds the hero—or heroine—of the day."

The horses kept sauntering.

Finally, a rider separated from the bunch, picked up a canter, and surged up and over a head-high brush fence and out of the ring. Mrs. Scott. Of course.

"Atta girl," Ralph breathed.

She and Cloud thundered across the field. They took the post-and-rail, then gobbled up the ground at a gallop heading to the first coop, then the next. They picked up speed. Up and over the stone wall. Another. Still galloping. Sailed across a ditch and open water trap, then turned and headed toward that unforgiving wall of brush and log.

"Mr. Ralph, you're squeezing too hard," whimpered Vivian. He was clutching her hand as he watched.

"Sorry, child." He pulled her hand up to his old lips and gave it a quick peck. "Just nervous."

I held my breath, feeling Cloud's surging stride in my soul as Mrs. Scott charged toward the Aiken. My heart pounded. If Cloud slipped, if he hesitated, he wouldn't have enough lift or momentum to fly across that brush pile and log. Nothing in that thick jump would give way if a horse crashed into it. One misstep and Mrs. Scott could get hurt bad. She might even . . . she could . . . oh God.

"C'mon, Miss Milly," Ralph murmured.

Cloud lifted off, soared, arced, and landed. Safe.

In the distance came a cry of sheer jubilation from Mrs. Scott: "Gooooood boy!"

I felt myself finally exhale and looked up at Ralph. "That . . . that was phenomenal. I can't believe she could—" I stopped short.

Ralph was crying. Tears were slipping from his eyes, disappearing into those ravines of wrinkles, then dripping off his saggy chin. "She's back," he murmured.

Mrs. Scott cantered away from the Aiken. She jumped the brush fence back into the ring and reined Cloud down to a trot, then a walk, his sides heaving as he eased back down to normal.

Her competitors in the arena applauded lightly. A handful of spectators in the grandstand even rose into a standing ovation.

Mrs. Scott lifted her top hat in salute, and then—I swear in total sass—she tipped it at that nasty Mr. Carlson.

"Ho-ho! Look at that. That girl always was nervy." Ralph chuckled, wiped his eyes, and blew his big old nose in a handkerchief. Then, with reverence and relief and unmistakable love in his voice, he said: "See that ride? That's because of you two. You opened up her heart again. And trust me, young'uns, it's a lionheart."

He turned to me. "Your turn now, missy."

Sunup was all tacked and ready when Mrs. Scott made it back to the stalls with Cloud. I was holding him by the reins, walking him to limber up. Rex trailed behind me, still carrying currycombs at the ready as if outside air might somehow dirty Sunup. I wanted to tell him not to worry, that he'd made Sunup gleam like a brand-new copper penny, and to thank him, but somehow the words stuck in my throat. I kept walking.

Watching us, Ralph just shook his head.

Mrs. Scott rode up to me. She had come in second, behind the movie theater lady. Which meant she didn't win the prize money. She dropped to the ground stiffly, putting her hand to her back with a grimace before loosening the girth and crossing her stirrups over the saddle. She really was a little old to be riding such a physically demanding course.

"I . . . I'm sorry you didn't win, Mrs. Scott. Your ride was . . . was . . ." I decided on Vivian's word, "A-mazing."

She shrugged. "Couldn't be helped. Evelyn's horse had tremendous scope. A relentless gallop and brilliant vault. Can't fight fact. I had just hoped to take some pressure off us with the cash prize." She patted Cloud. "You were absolutely lovely, even so, fella."

She handed Cloud's reins to Rex. "Please sponge him down and make sure he drinks a good amount of water."

Reluctantly, Rex left, Cloud in hand, throwing a backward look at me. I felt my face turn hot red.

Was this ever going to stop?

Seeing my blush, Mrs. Scott held that pointer finger up at me. No words necessary. She continued her matter-of-fact assessment. "I suspect winning will put Evelyn in a better mood for some haggling. I've already gotten a bit of a bidding war going between her and Paul for Caspian—thanks to you, Beatrice."

Mrs. Scott stripped off her riding gloves, her formal coat, and stock tie, and unbuttoned her collar with a sigh of relief. She finally looked as hot and sweaty as I felt. I had never, ever seen her like that. Even picking peaches. I stared. Worried about her suddenly. She . . . she wouldn't have a heart attack or something, would she?

Mrs. Scott caught me staring.

I snapped my gaze away, embarrassed, like I'd accidentally opened the bathroom door and caught her in her underwear.

With a self-conscious frown, she pushed her hair off from her face and tucked its waves back into the formal hairnet she'd used for the show.

Considered me for a moment. Started to say something, then stopped. Began and reined in again.

Finally nodding to herself, Mrs. Scott twisted off the odd, coarse ring made of a horseshoe nail that she always wore. "Ralph gave this to me the first show I rode in. For luck. It's always been very precious to me. I'd like you to have it now. Before you go into the arena with the chest—with Sunup." Mrs. Scott laid the iron-nail ring in my palm and added in a soft voice, "Sometimes life hands us family that has nothing to do with blood ties, Beatrice."

I caught my breath as I stared down at the ring. Out of nowhere Ralph's song—*it wouldn't be make-believe if you believed in me*—filled my mind. Foolish old man. Foolish to count on someone being there for you. Foolish to trust in family. And yet . . . My heart ached to believe Mrs. Scott meant what she was hinting at. And that hope felt like coming out of a cave into dazzling sunlight.

I slipped the ring onto my finger. It fit. Like it had been made for me.

We stood in awkward silence until Sunup tossed his head, snorted, and nudged me.

Mrs. Scott laughed. "Well, he seems ready. Let's go show them what you've done with this horse, shall we?"

CHAPTER 30

By then it was late afternoon. The sun was low in the sky as, once again, Mrs. Scott escorted me past the show's stalls on the way to the arena. Caspian had sauntered along, cool, collected, unruffled. Sunup, on the other hand, was tossing his head around, fighting the bit, raring to go. Like a racehorse. Or one about to spook.

"Sit back in the saddle. Relax your legs. Don't give him any cue to take off," Mrs. Scott cautioned me, putting her hand on his reins. "Easy, boy. Eeeeeea-sy."

Sunup slowed his walk a little to match hers, but I could still feel how coiled he was, how ready to spring. His neck was already lathered in anxiety sweat.

"Easy, boy. Eeeeeeea-sy," Mrs. Scott and I chorused.

Mrs. Scott looked up at the sky as we jigged along, and frowned. "The show is running late. The sun is going to cast long shadows off those fences, Beatrice, be sure to—"

"Are you kidding me?" A loud, annoyed voice interrupted her. "You're showing that horse? THAT horse?"

Sunup reared, ripping the rein from Mrs. Scott's guiding hand. Whinnied sharply. Thrashed his front legs.

I was so startled I didn't have time to grab his mane to keep myself from whipping around in the saddle. I'm not sure how I stayed on.

Sunup came back to the ground, then immediately reared again, throwing his head around wildly.

"Whoa, whoa now," Mrs. Scott managed to

grab his bridle's noseband and used her weight to swing him down and anchor him.

But Sunup kept snorting belligerently, pawing the ground, backing up, pulling her along, then lunging forward, pushing her around dangerously. She was going to get hurt.

"Let go, Mrs. Scott. I have him, I have him," I cried. "Whoa, Sunup. Whoa." I rubbed my hand reassuringly along his shoulders and withers as he thrashed. "It's all right. You're all right. Eeeeeeea-sy."

Finally, he stopped popping up and down as if he were trying to stomp a snake. But Sunup kept huffing in blasts, his nostrils wide and alarmed, and dancing around, his tail thrashing his sides and my legs.

Mrs. Scott's face turned steely as she turned around to the voice that had so alarmed Sunup. It was that nasty Mr. Carlson. "I see he recognizes you," she said quietly.

It was him? That was the man who'd scarred Sunup, kicking him brutally with sharp spurs? My beautiful Sunup? Oh, how I wished for a crop that I could let him have it. Right across his smug, mean face. Let him see how it felt.

She must have read my mind, because Mrs. Scott put a hand on my toes. "Eeeeeea-sy," she murmured.

Mr. Carlson's face was the color of his hunt jacket. "Are you trying to mock me by entering that worthless fleabag?"

"Mock you?" Mrs. Scott seemed genuinely surprised by the notion. "No. But . . . now that you mention it, Mr. Carlson, it certainly would be an added prize for the day." She patted my foot. "Come along, Beatrice." She marched us past Mr. Carlson without another look at him.

"You'll pay for this new insult, Mrs. Scott. I promise you," he shouted at her back.

We walked on for several minutes in silence, me shaking I was so angry.

When we reached the outside rim of the arena where riders were gathering, Mrs. Scott stopped and looked up at me. "Let go of that now," she warned me. "Being angry is a distraction."

"But he—"

She held up her pointer finger. "I know. Channel it into determination. All right?"

Grudgingly, I nodded. "How do you do it, Mrs. Scott?"

"What's that?"

"Keep yourself calm?"

She snorted—a most unladylike noise and very unlike her. "Trust me, Beatrice. I am rarely calm. Especially with a buffoon like that. I have just learned—the hard way—to hide it as best I can. And to let my actions speak for me. Right now, the action that will silence that idiot man and avenge Sunup is you and he doing well in this class." She smiled at me, flashing dimples and arching an eyebrow. "Not to ladle more pressure on you, of course."

She was joking. I didn't know Mrs. Scott could joke. I laughed—a little. But no matter what she said, I sure did feel even more pressure and responsibility. Now besides trying to save Mrs. Scott's farm, my little sister and me, even Ralph and Malachi and that annoying boy, Rex, I also needed to prove that Mr. Carlson was wrong about Sunup.

The first rider was called into the ring. She circled her horse, cleared the first fence—white-washed poles surrounded by potted geraniums—beautifully. Took the sharp turn between jumps four and five in perfect rhythm. Glided over a picket fence and approached the final obstacle—three simple rails. Easy-peasy. But the horse shied, ran out to the side, and refused.

The crowd groaned.

The rider tried again. Same thing. She left the arena without finishing the course.

"Shadows. See them?" Mrs. Scott whispered to me. The sun was casting one long ominous shadow from each rail, like black slats in the grass. Like cattle guards put in a road to stop cows from crossing.

The second rider had another perfect ride but then crashed through that final fence, scattering the poles across the ground. The third horse skidded to a halt and back-pedaled. The fourth dirty stopped, dumping his rider to the grass in front of the jump.

I panicked. "What do I do? What do I do?"

Mrs. Scott put her hand on my knee. "Keep your eyes on the top rail as you approach it. Don't look to the ground. Pick up speed off the seventh jump and let Sunup eat up the ground so he doesn't have time to pay any attention to the shadows. It means you might break out of a canter into a gallop, but that's all right. There's room after the fence for you to bring him back down."

"But don't I need to keep a nice, consistent pace?"

"If you are the only rider to go clean through the course it won't matter. This ride is going to be about heart and courage." She patted my leg. "And you are all that, Beatrice."

Three more riders—no one cleared that jump. The crowd had gone silent, watching nervously, no longer hoping to be wowed, just hoping to not have to witness a serious injury. Sunup had gotten so antsy, I had to keep circling him on the edge of the arena.

Another rider started through the gate, then seemed to change his mind, handing his number to the gate attendant, and withdrawing.

I was next.

Mrs. Scott nodded. "You can do this."

My heart galloping, I approached the arena's gate. Sunup swaggered in, head high, elated, full of happy anticipation at jumping anything the world put before him, just like the day he chased Charity and launched himself over stone walls for fun. I managed to control him enough to circle to find his canter, holding his excitement back, waiting for the judge's bell. And as I did, I caught sight of Mr. Carlson at the fence, talking to the banker, gesturing wildly. I circled again and saw him point toward Mrs. Scott. What was that villain saying?

The bell rang.

I set my jaw. "All right, boy," I murmured. "For Mrs. Scott."

I let Sunup burst forward. *Da-da-dum. Da-da-dum.* We came to the first jump and its edging of pretty geraniums. I lifted myself off his back into a crouch as he sprang up from the ground. Felt him tuck his front legs, round his back in a perfect arc, sail, sail, sail, and then unfold his legs to touch ground—so nimble, so elegant, so seemingly effortless that I wanted to cry in appreciation of the beauty of it.

Da-da-dum. Da-da-dum.

Over a combination. Over a double bar.

I stopped thinking about anything other than the fast-waltz rhythm of Sunup's hooves on the grass, the feel of his sheer joy.

We came to the picket fence, the last obstacle to get over before coming to the jump that no one had made. Sunup vaulted over, and as he landed, I gave him a looser rein, pressed my legs against his ribs—where that terrible man had once abused him—and felt Sunup flick his tail in a horse's watch-this bravado and surge forward, surge, surge.

Top rail. Keep your eye on the top rail. Don't look down, Sunup, don't look down. *Trust me.*

A few yards away. *Leg on. Leg on.* He quickened. Sunup's tail swished and snapped.

I felt him flex, coil himself for takeoff, and then we were up and flying.

Soaring—suspended in an exquisite, dazzling

show of the grace and power possible in a horse, and the generosity of his sharing it with a mere human, a rider he loves. For just a moment of heart-stopping bliss. Then down again to earth.

Clear! We'd done it!

We cantered away, me laughing in triumph, Sunup shaking his head exuberantly. And in that one glorious moment, I believed everything I hoped.

Copying what I did—copying me!—the last two adult riders also rode clear.

But we—a once beaten-up horse and beaten-down girl—we won.

Just like Malachi had predicted—Sunup's flashiness and scopey jump had impressed the judges. But evidently, I did too. They told me they'd never seen a girl with such gumption. And that our ride had been "poetry." They gave me the sweetest medallion of a bronze horse head decorating my blue ribbon. And fifty dollars! Fifty! I swear I floated out of the arena I was so astonished and relieved and exhilarated all at once.

But then I saw Mrs. Scott surrounded by the man she called Paul, the movie theater lady, the evil Mr. Carlson, and the banker. My heart sank. And I remembered what the outcome would be if Sunup actually won. He would be sold—saving us all—but forever gone.

Vivian came skipping, Rex behind her, and Ralph moving his old frame as fast as he could.

"You won, you won, you won, you won!" Viv singsonged.

"Dang, girl!" Rex beamed at me. "You rode those jumps faster than a hot knife goes through butter! And looked darn good doing it."

"Shoo," Ralph said to him.

"Aww, Grandpop!"

Ralph put his hand on my knee. "That was mighty fine riding, young'un. Mighty fine."

"What's going on over there?" I asked, nodding my head toward the knot of people surrounding Mrs. Scott.

"Oh, that man has his knickers all in a knot, claiming Mrs. Scott tricked him into giving up this horse. But no one's believing him, child. Don't you worry. And the other three are nearly knocking one another over trying to outbid t'other."

Watching, I blinked back tears.

Finally, Mr. Carlson stormed away. Mrs. Scott shook everyone else's hands and headed toward us.

"Beatrice, that was magnificent. Congratulations and"—she put her hand to her heart and bowed her head—"thank you. I have paid my mortgage and my taxes—for this entire year. And it's all because of you."

Once I would have given just about anything for those compliments from Mrs. Scott, but now they rolled right off me in my sadness about losing Sunup. Still, I was sticking to our agreement. I wouldn't complain. Or beg to keep him, despite my soul crying out to ask. "So . . . what happens now?"

"Caspian will go to Paul and school his daughter-in-law across the hunt field. He wanted Cloud as well, but Evelyn doubled what Paul offered." Mrs. Scott smiled. "Evelyn caught onto the fact that Paul and I might have staged his offer on Cloud, betting that she'd outdo him. She found it amusing as long as I promised to do the same for her someday." Mrs. Scott nodded. "I think I'm going to enjoy working with her."

I took a deep breath. "What . . . what about—"

"Sunup, the New Deal Horse? Evelyn offered the whole thousand dollars she won in the stakes' outside course class for him." Mrs. Scott turned to Ralph. "Told me that was easy enough, that's what she paid on bootlegged champagne for her last party!"

Ralph let out a long whistle.

"So . . . he's going to the heiress?" I asked, my lip quivering despite my resolve. At least that meant I might be able to see him.

Mrs. Scott approached and stroked Sunup's nose. "No. The sale of Caspian and Cloud were enough to cover my debts until late spring. Paul and Evelyn and the banker all hired me to work with their horses as trainer, which hopefully means next year will be better for us. Besides . . ." She paused and looked up at me, arching an eyebrow. "Some horses are meant to be one-person ponies.

Given what Sunup once endured with that jackass and what you've coaxed out of him? And the gorgeous way you two just rode—together—on that course? I think you might just qualify for the National Horse Show next year. If we compete you the whole season to gather enough points, starting in June. You'd be the first teenage girl to try it."

She held up that pointer finger. "It will take an enormous amount of training. You game?"

"Yes, ma'am!" I almost shouted.

"All right, then." She nodded. Smiled—the best smile yet. "Let's go home."

Home.

I rubbed my thumb along the horseshoe-nail ring, turning it around my finger. The ring Ralph had given Mrs. Scott long ago, and she had now passed on to me.

Home.

"Yes, ma'am!" I clucked to Sunup. "Walk on, boy."

We followed Mrs. Scott, her old stable hand, his grandson, and my little sister, skipping and yanking on Ralph's hand to hurry him, chirping that she could hardly wait to describe everything she'd seen that day to Malachi. All of them troubled by things life had doused them in. Me on a horse that had had to fight through past wrongs, through his fear and anger, to trust me.

A new family, a new deal.

I thought back to waking up in a hayloft, hungry, grimy, abandoned. And to one of the first tunes I heard Ralph singing, about shaking off the blues and coming out of shadows, to no longer being afraid—all because someone coaxed the singer into believing.

Life can be so sweet on the sunny side of the street.

And just like Mrs. Scott, I smiled—the best smile yet.

AUTHOR'S NOTE AND THANKS

> *"Out of every crisis, every tribulation,*
> *every disaster, mankind rises with*
> *some share of greater knowledge, of*
> *higher decency, of purer purpose."*
> *—President Franklin Delano Roosevelt*

I was blessed to grow up surrounded by adults who had survived the Depression and World War II. The people we call the Greatest Generation. Even as a child, I was awed by their no-nonsense resiliency, their matter-of-fact sense of responsibility to help others get back on their feet when they needed it, in a pervasive *there but for the grace of God* attitude.

They hailed from all corners of the community:

garden club ladies who ran constant philanthropic drives to those who worked the land and helped nurse their neighbor's livestock through sudden life-threatening calamity in the middle of stormy nights. Townspeople embroiled in homegrown politics about things like adding stop signs or beautifying roadsides with daffodils or expanding the library. Elders who recounted history in colorful, often wry anecdotes about ordinary people who'd met harsh challenges thrown at them by global events with unwavering devotion to family and extraordinary pluck, ingenuity, or endearing stubbornness.

The type of people who got us through some of the darkest chapters of American history. And the Great Depression was decidedly one of those.

How did it happen? In brief: The fast, exuberant economic growth known as "the Roaring Twenties," came to a horrible halt in 1929. Leading up to that, a booming economy made the stock market seem an easy, quick way to make a fortune. Everyone wanted to get on the proverbial bandwagon, driving stock prices even higher, often inflated far beyond what a company was worth.

Banks made risky loans, counting on quick turnaround. Businesses began producing more items than consumers wanted. That started stock prices dipping, then jumping up again, in roller-coaster swings. But no one heeded the warning.

On October 24, stock prices took a nosedive. Then five days later, on what became known as "Black Tuesday," the markets crashed. Panicked selling by investors only made the plummet worse. Billions of dollars of savings evaporated in one disastrous day. Stocks that people had purchased at fifty dollars per share—often on credit, meaning they had taken out mortgages on their homes or farms or shops—were now lucky to be sold at fifty cents. Within months, businesses around the nation faltered and closed, laying off workers. Families lost their homes and farms to banks because they could no longer make their payments. Unable to collect owed money from suddenly destitute Americans and mobbed by depositors rushing their doors, banks failed, so citizens who actually did have money in their savings accounts could not get their cash. Tax revenues fell, meaning teachers were laid off, and many public schools closed.

By 1932, one out of every four Americans were out of work, unable to find even odd jobs. Twenty-eight percent had no income at all. Many took to the road looking for temporary crop-picking jobs. Others in the city existed in encampments of tar-paper huts, pointedly dubbed "Hoovervilles."

One out of every five preschool and school-aged children were suffering malnutrition. Many families, desperate to feed and clothe their children, "farmed them out," as Bea and Vivian's father did, sending them to relatives or family friends who seemed in better circumstances—even if only slightly.

That year, presidential candidate Franklin Delano Roosevelt promised voters "a new deal for the American people" and "action now." When accepting his party's nomination, FDR said: "The greatest tribute that I can pay to my countrymen is that in these days of crushing want there persists an orderly and hopeful spirit on the part of the millions of our people who have suffered so much. To fail to offer them a new chance is not only to betray their hopes but to misunderstand their patience. . . . This is no time for fear, for reaction or for timidity. . . . Statesmanship and vision, my friends, require relief to all at the same time. . . . Let us use common sense and business sense. . . . In so doing, employment can be given to a million men. . . . This Nation is not merely a Nation of independence, but it is, if we are to survive, bound to be a Nation of interdependence—town and city, and North and South, East and West. . . . Let us all here assembled constitute ourselves prophets of a new order of competence and of courage."

In his first one hundred days after taking office on March 4, 1933, FDR kickstarted programs to address unemployment, initiating agencies like the Works Progress Administration (WPA)—hiring 8.5 million people to construct bridges, public buildings, and roads—and the Civilian Conservation Corps (CCC) that put young men, seventeen to twenty-five years of age, to work in national parks, planting trees, building campgrounds, and fighting fires. The first CCC camp opened in Virginia's George Washington National Forest, just six weeks after FDR's inauguration. Its workers were housed, fed, clothed, and paid $30 a month—$25 of that sent home to their families. Many of the youth had been living on the streets and illiterate. They were taught to read and write in the camps.

One of the greatest joys of being an author is constantly learning new things—even on topics I thought I knew fairly well. Which was definitely the case while researching Bea's world, its 1930s timeframe, and its horse community.

Mrs. Scott, for instance—like most multifaceted and compelling characters—is an amalgamation. She was inspired by a number of Virginia horsewomen I was delighted to learn more about. They included Isabel Dodge Sloane, who in 1934 became the first woman to lead the American owners' list when one of her colts won the Kentucky Derby and another the Preakness. Charlotte Noland, a charismatic foxhunter, who believed young women should be both fit and well-educated and started the renowned girls-only Foxcroft School. A Middleburg widow who ran a seventy-stall stable and horse-breaking and trading operation, known for having one of the "keenest eyes for horses in the area."

"Strong, independent businesswomen," as one of the essayists in the wonderful *Horse Girls* aptly describes seasoned horse trainers, "who demonstrate affection by raising jumps and taking away your stirrups. . . . Unsentimental about horses but devoted to them for life," women exuding instinctive, second-nature "old-school feminism."

Women I so admire and to whom I am so indebted as a mother. I watched such women coax my daughter out of shyness into an extraordinarily poised competitive rider, a United States Pony Club (USPC) champion eventer. In that world she was blessed to find Karen Nutt, a lovingly honest and fiercely supportive trainer, plus the most wondrous self-possessed, anything-but-silly, mutually encouraging peer group of teenage equestrians. Coaches, role models, and teammates that parents dream of.

Lastly, the Evelyn Corker character is based on the bodacious Elizabeth Whitney Person Lunn Tippett, champion hunter show rider who made it to the National Horse Show on several horses, as well as an owner/breeder of racehorses. In 1939, *Time* magazine described her as a "spirited, devil-may-care rider . . . her drawing-room, gum-chewing, social-worker hairdo, haphazard clothes aped by many lesser socialites" . . . her horses "the envy of the show ring."

A Philadelphia native and model for Pond's face cream, her first husband, "Jock" Whitney, did indeed purchase her a 2,200-acre, million-dollar estate as his wedding present in 1930. He was one of the many industrialists, railroad tycoons, and financiers from New York and New England, who discovered the rolling, lush landscape of Fauquier and Loudoun counties, bought and refurbished old estates that had fallen on hard times, adding a monied patina to the area's foxhunting tradition. One of those stark dichotomies between the haves and have-nots that existed during the Great Depression.

Malachi is representative of the brave African Americans who served in World War I, fighting on Europe's front lines in the segregated 92nd and 93rd Infantry Divisions. Some, like the 369th Regiment, known as the Harlem Hellfighters, were assigned to the French Army in April 1918, fighting in harrowing battles such as the Meuse-Argonne Offensive. One hundred and seventy of them received France's much honored Croix de Guerre medal for bravery.

These veterans returned to the United States expecting their courage under fire and their service to bring them more equality back home. Tragically, this was not the case. They met a backlash of racism and resentment from whites—friction that boiled up into what was one of the most violent periods in American history, the "Red Summer" of 1919 when race riots rocked twenty-six cities across the United States. Some Black veterans were even attacked as their communities held parades to honor their service overseas—which is what I imagined happened to Malachi, causing his impaired vision.

By contrast, the "Bonus Army" of 1932 was a stunning model of integration and joint acceptance. Thousands of veterans—white and Black—from across the nation, marched together to Washington, DC, to lobby Congress for a bonus that had been promised to be delivered in 1945. (Compensation for the income they'd lost during their time fighting overseas—like back wages.) But given the Depression's financial devastation, the veterans needed the money then rather than later.

Patriotic and hopeful, they massed quietly and kept vigil by the Capitol as Congress deliberated, many of them bringing their children along to witness history. They camped in nearby Anacostia, creating an impressively organized mini town of tents and quickly-built cabins. They divided it into small streets named for states. The Salvation Army ran a library in its middle. Each night the veterans and their families gathered for music—gospel, blues, country, popular—Blacks and whites listening and performing together. Visitors were astonished by the two races peacefully and happily sharing billets, chores, and rations.

Local authorities and the regular army, however, saw the veterans' growing numbers and integrated cooperation as threatening, motivated and manipulated by "subversive," socialist or communist ideology. The House passed the bill. But when the Senate voted it down, President Hoover sent in troops to drive the Bonus Army out of Washington and destroy their encampment—even though the veterans had already dispersed themselves, despite their shocked disappointment, still singing "America the Beautiful."

For many, this cruelty was the last straw in the Hoover administration's disregard for the plight of the average American. They turned their attention and support to the then relatively unknown progressive democrat FDR.

I introduce my readers to his New Deal by mention of a rally held in Leesburg the summer of 1932 that was indeed spearheaded by a young female attorney—(a few brave mavericks did exist in the 1920s and 30s!)—that my character Dr. Liburn attends. His bio, by the way, echoes the real-life Maurice Britton King Edmead Sr., a doctor from the island of Saint Kitts, who, despite being refused hospital admitting rights because of the color of his skin, practiced and tended patients in Loudoun County for two decades. A graduate of the famed HBCU Howard University, Dr. Edmead was an ardent activist for improving Virginia's education for African American students when school segregation was the rule.

Most of us know about the horrors of the Dust Bowl in the Midwest that destroyed farms and set thousands of people onto the road looking for work and shelter. (If you have not read John Steinbeck's heart-wrenching *Grapes of Wrath* or Karen Hesse's *Out of the Dust*, please do.) I am embarrassed to say I didn't know about the 1930 and 1932 droughts that brought rural Virginia to its knees. Today, in our twenty-first century of dams, city reservoirs, and bottled water we don't really know the kind of fear and utter devastation drought can bring. In 1930, creeks and wells ran completely dry. Without any water—in Virginia counties that were the largest dairy producers in the nation—cattle had to be slaughtered or shipped out at terrible losses to their farmers. Corn came up, only grew knee-high, and died before tasseling. The brutal, rainless summer heat scorched grazing pastures, ravaged hay fields, cut the apple harvest in half.

Dr. Chatman the rainmaker came about because of my noticing a teeny note on a map that ran in a November 1930 *Fortune* magazine article about the transplanting of the Long Island hunt set to Virginia. Evidently, these foxhunters were despairing over the fact the ground was so hard and dry their hounds couldn't catch the scent of foxes they hoped to chase.

It read: "So serious was the 1930 drought that fox-hunters tried last month to commission Dr. G.I.A.M. Sykes, professional rainmaker. Suggested price: $12,000." My mouth dropped at the amount—$12,000 in 1930? (That's equal to about $182,000 in today's dollars.)

Thanks to the kindness and research expertise of the historical collection librarians at Leesburg's Thomas Balch Library, I was able to read obscure local and academic articles about Dr. Skyes's large personality and made-up pseudoscientific vocabulary, as well as other outlandish "pluviculturists" of the time.

Which leads nicely to other heartfelt thanks: Historian and writer Jessica Serfilippi—whom I first met while working on *Hamilton and Peggy! A Revolutionary Friendship*—did some quick research for me that is so representative of the necessary work needed in responsible period pieces—determining what is factual and, therefore, plausible to use. Most of the research she did is invisible, providing enriching backstory for characters like Malachi, but also telling me I couldn't have

FDR make a train-stop stump speech in Leesburg, even though he did stop at several nearby rail stations as he campaigned in Virginia. No matter how much I wanted to write such a scene, FDR just wasn't there!

As always, my adult children, Peter and Megan, exquisitely gifted writing and theater professional artists, were my steadfast, uplifting muses, my trusted go-to "writers' colony" for feedback on narrative pacing, themes, character, my unflinching "horse trainers" in their honest, adroit critiques and unwavering confidence in me. To Sara Schonfeld for her nuance and painstaking watchfulness during copy editing. And, of course, to Katherine Tegen, a true virtuoso editor, unparalleled in her literary vision and generous devotion to those she believes in. Katherine has trusted me to write ten novels for her, exploring topics as divergent as the young poet who was Leonardo's first portrait in fifteenth-century Florence to the Revolutionary War's Peggy Schuyler to a downed pilot trying to evade Nazis to a young teen perplexed by anti-Vietnam war protests. Few authors enjoy such a nurturing, longstanding editorial relationship, and I am intensely grateful for it.

SELECTED SOURCES:

Blumenthal, Karen. *Six Days in October: The Stock Market Crash of 1929*. New York: Atheneum Books for Young Readers, 2002.

Favreau, Marc. *Crash: The Great Depression and the Fall and Rise of America*. New York: Little Brown Books for Young Readers, 2018.

Freedman, Russell. *Children of the Great Depression*. New York: Houghton Mifflin Harcourt, 2005.

Mullenbach, Cheryl. *The Great Depression for Kids: Hardship and Hope in 1930s America*. Chicago: Chicago Review Press, 2015.

Perdue, Charles L. and Nancy J. Martin, editors. *Talk About Trouble: A New Deal Portrait of Virginians in the Great Depression*. Chapel Hill, NC: The University of North Carolina Press, 1996.

Terkel, Studs. *Hard Times: An Oral History of the Great Depression*. New York: The New Press, 2005.

Uys, Errol Lincoln. *Riding the Rails: Teenagers on the Move in the Great Depression*. Boston: T. E. Winter & Sons, 2014.

FEATURE BIOPIC FILMS:

Ross, Gary, director. *Seabiscuit*, Universal Pictures, 2003.

Howard, Ron, director. *Cinderella Man*, Universal Pictures, 2005.

Washington, Denzel, director. *The Great Debaters*, MGM, 2007.

Sargent, Joseph, director. *Warm Springs*, HBO, 2005.

DOCUMENTARIES:

PBS: The American Experience: FDR

PBS: The American Experience: The 1930s

PBS Ken Burns: The Dust Bowl